A PRIVATE AFFAIR

A.C. ARTHUR

MILLS & BOON

A PRIVATE AFFAIR

AC ARTHUR

CHAPTER ONE

MILLS & BOON

CHAPTER ONE

Milan, Italy

RILEY GOLD DIDN'T give a damn. She walked into the hotel ballroom knowing she was the best-dressed woman in the room.

Her dress was an RGold exclusive—black sheath, skew neck, half sleeve, back slit. The shoes were Louboutin crisscross pumps. Her shoulder-length honey-bronze highlighted hair was pulled up in a slick bun that had taken thirty minutes to perfect. Her makeup was simple, with dark eyes and matte berry-toned lips.

She was ready for the New Year's Eve party sponsored by *Design International*—a global magazine that routinely featured the hottest designers worldwide. As the chief executive of market research and product development at Ronald Gold Fashions, Riley was representing the company at this party, even though she was on her annual vacation.

RGF was on top of the domestic fashion market

and holding strong at the top five in the global market. The company her grandfather had built and her father now ran was everything to Riley. It was her life, as the tabloids never failed to remind everyone.

RGF's Ice Princess Still as Frigid as Ever

That was the latest headline. A picture of her walking into RGF's Manhattan headquarters beneath it. Riley could still see the bold-print letters splashed across the front of the magazine as if they'd been emblazoned on the insides of her eyelids. Despite the headline and the article she refused to read, Riley had taken extreme pride in the classy dove-gray pantsuit she'd been wearing in the picture. She'd learned a long time ago that appearances were everything. It didn't matter if she felt like crap, as long as she was flawless on the outside.

Flawless and brilliant.

Riley crossed the room, smiling and waving at industry people she knew. She stopped for a quick double-cheek air kiss with an international textile associate and provided vague answers to a fashion blogger's questions about what RGF had in store for New York Fashion Week. Her target was in sight and she was steadily making her way toward him—without looking as if she'd only come to this party to see him. Admittedly, he was a big part of the reason, but she didn't have to act like it.

There had to be at least three hundred people in

the hotel's massive ballroom. A band played while staff weaved in and out of the guests with trays of hors d'oeuvres and flutes filled with champagne. Glitz and glamour were the theme on this New Year's Eve, with some of the top names in fashion wearing signature gowns and tuxedos. The air buzzed with excitement—for the New Year as well as the upcoming fashion season.

Riley was excited about the latter, as well. A lot was riding on the top-secret Golden Bride couture collection. This was the first major project Riley had worked on in the three years after the colossal mess she'd made of an international distribution deal that should have been a slam dunk.

Her assistant, Korey, had learned that up-and-coming designer Perry Reddleson would be attending this party. Ron Gold, Jr., CEO and lead designer at RGF, wanted Perry on his team. Riley had vowed to make her father proud by convincing Perry to work for the company. She'd practiced her pitch at least a hundred times during the flight here and again in her suite as she'd dressed for tonight. Now was the moment of truth.

"Perry Reddleson, I didn't expect to see you here," she said, coming to a stop in front of him.

He was a slim man with a head of sandy-brown curls that fell to his shoulders. His signature black frame glasses and dimples were on full display as he grinned back at her.

"The impeccable Riley, so very lovely to see you here in the city of fashion," he replied. He snagged two glasses from the tray that was being carried past and offered her one.

Riley accepted the glass and launched into her pitch. Twenty minutes and another glass of champagne later, Perry was grinning as he said, "All you had to do was ask. I'd be honored to talk about the possibility of joining the RGF empire."

He had a nice smile, Riley supposed. She was more concerned with the answer he'd just given her. It earned him a genuine smile from her, even as she began thinking of how fast she could head back to her room. The job she'd come to do was done, and more than anything else, she was ready for some time alone. To unwind and just be herself. Something, she thought as her fingers moved over the stem of the empty glass she held, that she never had enough time to do.

"You won't regret it," Riley told him. "RGF is more than its reputation. We pride ourselves on keeping a family-oriented work environment. If you were to officially join us, you wouldn't be just another designer—you'd be family."

He chuckled. "You don't have to continue to sell me on the offer, Riley. I've been following RGF's success for a long time. And I'm honored that the Ice Princess herself came all this way just to speak to me. There's no way I would turn down this opportunity."

Riley hated being called the Ice Princess. The tabloids had given her that nickname after the Walter Stone fiasco. And while she wasn't about to give Perry a tongue-lashing for using the stupid name, she did raise a brow as she stared at him. The act had Perry laughing loudly as if she'd just told a fabulous joke.

"Just kidding, Riley. Come on, let's dance," Perry said.

He plucked the glass from her fingers and placed it, with his own, on the next tray to pass them. He was taking her hand before Riley could cordially turn down his offer and in seconds she found herself on the dance floor.

The song wasn't a slow tune, which meant he really didn't need to hold her so closely. Yet Riley didn't pull away. She was certain any one of the media staff that were present would snap a picture on their phone and immediately text it to their editor. The picture of her dancing with Perry would no doubt grace the cover of at least one tabloid first thing tomorrow morning. Any other fashion house looking to snag Perry's talent would see that RGF had beaten them to the punch. With that thought, Riley moved easily to the rhythm of the music. She smiled and eased out of Perry's embrace so she could spin around before coming back to join Perry. The move gave anyone aiming for a photo op an unfettered view of her smiling…and wearing an RGold original dress.

Another minute and the song was over. The band would probably continue to play until midnight when the DJ, who was set up in the far corner of the ballroom, would take over. Riley still hoped to be upstairs in bed by that time. Now she decided it was time to conclude this meeting.

"Well, I certainly don't wish to stop your celebrating," she said and dropped her hands from his shoulders. "I appreciate you taking the time to speak to me."

Perry let his hands slip from her waist. "Surely you're not leaving the party. We still have an hour to go until midnight. There's champagne to drink and more dancing to be done!"

Riley smiled at the joy in his sea green eyes. "Oh no, I think I've had enough partying for one evening," she told him.

"Nonsense," a deep voice said from behind her. "You have to make time for just one more dance."

Riley's shoulders instantly stiffened at the familiar voice.

"You don't mind, do you, Perry?" he asked as he shook Perry's hand.

"Of course not," Perry replied. "As long as she continues to have a good time. We should all be on the dance floor at midnight. I'll be talking to you soon, Riley."

She managed a quiet good-night to Perry, her genuine smile already shifting to the cool, aloof one she'd grown famous for.

This time, the band did begin playing a slower tune, and to her dismay, Chadwick Warren stepped closer and asked, "Shall we dance?"

Riley didn't like how close he was.

Nor did she like how well he wore that single-button charcoal-gray tuxedo. Chaz, as everybody called him, was too tall, standing beyond even her older brother RJ's six feet two inches. His face was too chiseled, eyebrows too thick and beard cut too precisely. There were waves in his close-cropped ebony hair, too many of them, and he smelled... Well, the cologne he wore smelled too damn good.

There was no way Riley would ever let on that she was bothered by any of the above. She nodded and took the final step to close the distance between them.

"You look stunning tonight," he said the moment his arms slipped around her waist, his hands flattening at the small of her back.

For the second time tonight, Riley lifted her arms to let her hands rest on a man's shoulders. The first time had been for business. This time, she prayed, would not overshadow the work she'd just completed.

"Thank you," she replied. "You're wearing the Crew, from King Designs's winter collection. It's an excellent cut that wears well, even if a modern cut would have worked better."

The color of the tux also added to the intense look in his deep brown eyes.

He chuckled. "I'll take that as a compliment."

For a split second Riley thought she could become lost in his soulful eyes. She wondered how it would feel to run her fingers over his rich mocha-hued skin. That was ridiculous. She didn't shake her head to clear the thoughts and remind herself of who and what he was, but she did shift her gaze to a woman across the room wearing a blue sequin gown. Again, they were most certainly surrounded by reporters, bloggers and photographers, so Riley's smile stayed in place as she concentrated on moving with the music, instead of the fact that she was dancing with the enemy.

"Seeing you like this is a pleasant surprise," Chaz said after a few moments of silence.

"I've spent every New Year's Eve in Milan for the last three years," she responded before snapping her lips shut. He did not need to know anything that personal about her.

Chaz looked down at her seriously.

"You don't usually dance at parties was what I meant," he said.

He was right. She did not dance at parties. Whatever events Riley attended were carefully selected and always related to RGF business in some way. She would not admit that the last thing she'd wanted to do tonight was attend this party. If she'd been able to do exactly as she'd wanted, Riley would be upstairs in her room with a cup of hot chocolate and a tray of Oreo cookies—her favorite guilty pleasure. She would be in bed wearing her pajamas and watching some old holiday movie. That would have been the perfect way to bring in the New Year.

And if she'd been able to do that, instead of attending this party, she would have missed seeing him. Riley was definitely okay with that. She'd first met Chaz when she was seventeen at a fashion show in Miami. Years went by where she only caught stories about him either via office gossip or the media. And then last year he moved back to New York.

"I had a meeting with Perry," she told him, and took a step back, letting her hands slide down his chest and torso until they were once again at her sides.

He looked at her quizzically this time. "The song's not over."

"But I'm done," she replied.

He released his hold on her and gave a slight nod. "Like Cinderella running from the ball before the stroke of midnight."

Riley lifted her chin. "I don't believe in fairy tales."

CHAPTER TWO

Damn.

That woman could wear a bedsheet and she'd still be the sexiest lady he'd ever set eyes on. Too bad she was public enemy number one. Or rather, her family—the Golds—were the archenemy of Chaz's uncle, Tobias King. Chaz had been inducted into the feud via his parents' deaths when he was nine years old. And again a year ago when family loyalty insisted he take a leave of absence from his thriving social media consultation business to help rebrand and boost sales for the men's line at King Designs.

All of that came second to the fact that each time he'd been in the company of Riley Gold this past year, she'd treated him like he was part of the Republic and she was a high-ranking official with the Resistance. The thought made Chaz smile, even when his body had already begun to react to seeing her in that tight black dress.

She looked dangerous, desirable and just a little bit frightening. Like a badass goddess in five-inch heels.

Chaz brought the glass to his lips and took a sip of aged whiskey while keeping his gaze leveled on her. She stood across the room, near a highboy table decorated to match the room's gold-and-black decor. Her hair, which Chaz preferred loose and dancing over her shoulders, was pulled up so that the slender line of her neck was visible. Diamonds sparkled at her ears and matched the triple-tier bracelet on her left wrist. The skewed-neck design of the dress left one delectable tawny-hued shoulder bared, its tight fit outlining the perfection of her curves. Chaz took another swallow from his glass and convinced himself that the fixation he'd had on Riley Gold, for longer than he cared to admit, wasn't at all foolish or immature.

The man she was speaking to offered her a drink and she accepted, but she would not sip from that glass. If he was correct, and Chaz was ninety-eight percent certain he was, the glass was filled with scotch. Riley did not drink hard liquor. Champagne and red wine were her preference, as were desserts over any other portion of a meal. The fact that he knew those things and too many more to count was probably a little obsessive, but nobody had to know that but him.

"See something you like?"

Chaz didn't blink at the heavily Italian-accented voice. He did spare a glance to his right, where Franco Vitali now stood.

"I see several things of interest," Chaz replied.

Franco chuckled. "Even if you were not their biggest competitor in the US, she would not give you the time of day. Her heart has been frozen since the scandal years ago."

"Not my concern," Chaz told him. "I like variety."

He did—normally. Chaz had a general affection for women and gave them his time as the need arose. Which, for the last ten years, seemed to be quite often. Starting with a simple bachelor blog, Chaz had quickly built a social media following that consisted mainly of women trying their best to end his lone-star status. He'd parlayed that success into Conversation Media, a multimillion-dollar social media consulting firm that Chaz was extremely proud to own. Riley, on the other hand, occupied another space in his mind. One he had yet to figure out.

"Me, too," Franco continued. "Listen, there are dozens of models in my suite. They could not come down as they were not invited. You, my friend, are invited to join me upstairs to bring in the New Year properly."

Chaz managed a bland grin in Franco's direction. He'd known the guy for years, as he was one of Italy's most talented designers. And he had an eye for good art, just like Chaz. But Chaz had never partied with Franco.

"I think I'm good with my own celebration," Chaz said.

Franco shrugged his slim shoulders. "Suit yourself, *compagno*."

Alone once again, Chaz looked across the room only to be disappointed. Riley was gone. It was just as well. At least he'd had a partial dance with her. There could never be anything between them, anyway. His uncle, the feud, his new position at King Designs and the pending success of Chaz's new venture—ChatMe, a social media platform designed for on-the-go millennials enjoying the single life—stood in the way.

That meant Chaz had better things to do than to nurse thoughts about Riley Gold. He could save those for when he was alone in bed, as he'd been far too often to admit. Finishing his drink, Chaz decided he had time for one more business connection before the New Year rolled in. He was heading toward a well-known fashion magazine editor when he caught a glimpse of that infamous black dress and those long, sexy legs.

Chaz knew he shouldn't do it. He should continue his trek toward the editor, share a drink and small talk with her while dropping subtle hints about the new men's collection being debuted at Fashion Week. He should ignore Riley Gold the same way she always tried to ignore him.

But he didn't.

He couldn't. Which made no sense at all. Chaz never chased a woman.

To be fair, he wasn't actually doing so now. He was just walking toward the balcony. There was no rule against a man deciding to get some air...in the place that a beautiful woman was doing the same. And it wasn't because each time he'd seen her tonight she'd been with another man—two other men—who had been standing very close to her. That definitely wasn't the reason he stepped onto the balcony, because Chaz was not inclined to be jealous of anyone.

She was on the phone with her back to him.

He should walk away now. Just let her do what she did best: freeze people—or rather, him—out for no reason. It was tempting as he stood there and thrust his hands into the front pockets of his pants. There were still plenty of women in the ballroom who he could dance with, have drinks with while the New Year rolled in and maybe even take upstairs to his room for the night. He also hadn't forgotten Franco's offer to attend his private party. Again, plenty of willing women. Chaz did not have to stand here and deal with Riley Gold.

But the moment he heard the small hitch in her voice as she'd yelled at whoever she was speaking to, he knew he wasn't going up to any private party. And he wasn't going to snag some other woman from the ballroom. He was going to stay right here until he knew Riley was okay.

"Yes," she continued. "I told him that."

She was nodding while holding the cell phone to

her ear, as if the person she was speaking to could somehow see her.

"I said that, too. Look, RJ, you really didn't have to call. You should be getting ready for Uncle Harry's New Year's Eve party, and not worrying about whether or not I could close the deal. Which, as a matter of fact, I did. Perry will be in New York on January 5 to meet with you and Dad."

So this was about business. She was speaking to Ronald Gold III, better known as RJ, next in line to sit on the throne at RGF. Chaz almost turned back at that point. Riley's business was RGF's business and that did not involve him. He should have known the only thing causing any type of emotional reaction in her would have to do with her family company. All she ever did was work.

"Yes. Thank you. Happy New Year to you, too," she finished before pulling the phone away from her ear and disconnecting the call.

The wish she'd offered her brother was filled with frustration, and Chaz watched as she leaned over, resting her elbows on the railing. Straight ahead were the Duomo cathedral and glittering lights of the Milanese skyline. A gorgeous sight to behold. But Riley lowered her head and sighed.

Chaz had never seen her this way. Riley Gold was a fierce, intelligent woman who had proved herself as one of the most talented and shrewd businesswomen he'd ever met. If she had a weakness, no one would ever know what it was. If she faltered, nobody would ever witness it. She was gorgeous and on point every second of every day. Until now.

His first instinct was to walk right up, wrap his arms around her waist and revel in the feel of her back pressed against him. He would remind her that there was a time for business and a time for pleasure. Then he would drop a soft kiss on her temple and continue to hold her until she cuddled into his embrace. Then he would…

Chaz cleared his throat and pushed those ridiculous thoughts out of his mind. "Working on New Year's Eve?" he asked, still standing a short distance away from her.

She jumped, her elbows slipping on the railing so that it appeared she might fall. Chaz didn't hesitate. He hurried over, wrapping his arm around her waist in the same way he'd just been contemplating, and pulled her back against him.

"It's okay," he whispered against her temple. "I've got you now."

For a split second Riley enjoyed the comfortable warmth that engulfed her. But when his breath whispered over her skin and the reality of who he was and where they were hit her, she quickly moved out of his grasp.

"What are you doing?" she asked as she spun

around to face him. "Were you eavesdropping on my conversation? Is that why you were sent to this party?"

While her father liked to entertain conspiracy theories about company espionage, Riley prided herself on being a bit more levelheaded. Besides, Chaz had only worked in brand management for King Designs for the past year. It wouldn't be his job to hire a new designer, if he even knew enough about the industry to do so. But he had followed her out here for a reason.

"I was concerned when you left the party and I wanted to make sure you were all right," he said and casually folded his arms across his chest.

His legs were slightly spread, so that he looked formidable and enticing all at once. It appeared to be a practiced move—no doubt it was intended to make women swoon because it had a Morris Chestnut feel to it. The fact that Morris was one of Riley's favorite actors had to be the reason she thought Chaz looked so good standing there.

Riley cleared her throat.

"I'm fine," she said evenly. "Thank you for your concern, but you can leave now."

He smiled. A slow and potent action that had her clenching the phone and her purse just a little tighter.

Riley had no idea why this was always her reaction to him. He was just a man, after all. She interacted with a lot of men on a daily basis. There was nothing about Chaz Warren that made him any different from the others. Except maybe the fact that his family was her family's longest and most detested rival. Still, that never stopped her from reacting to his presence, no matter how hard she tried not to. Even now, the heat that always suffused every part of her when he was around was creeping to the surface. She felt it in her cheeks, in the way her breasts grew fuller and her center began that slow, needy pulsating.

"Not until I'm satisfied you're not going to jump over the railing because you don't like your family checking up on your work," he replied.

"What? Oh, so you *were* eavesdropping," she said and frowned.

"You weren't exactly whispering."

"It was nothing. And as I stated before, I'm fine," she said evenly.

Riley took another step back, but not in retreat. She told herself it was self-preservation, something she was very good at.

"Are you afraid of me, Riley?"

Her response was an immediate chuckle. "Don't be ridiculous," she replied and attempted to walk around him.

He blocked her path. He didn't touch her but stood directly in front of her. His gaze was dark and intense, deep brown eyes and thick neat brows staring down at her. Riley didn't look away.

"You've no place to run this time," he said, his voice going lower. Sexier.

She remained unfazed, at least on the outside. "I don't run from anything," she told him. "And I'm not easily intimidated."

He tilted his head curiously and arched a brow. "Good. Now we can finally get this out of the way."

He took another step and leaned in before pausing to look down at her hands. Riley had not moved a muscle. She held eye contact with him. A part of her wanted to take another step around him, while another part—the stubborn and inquisitive part—stood still and waited. For what, she wasn't quite sure. All she knew for certain was that she wanted to know what he was going to do next—almost as much as she wanted Perry Reddleston to come work for RGF.

"Is that a yes?" he asked.

"I didn't say anything," she replied.

"Exactly," he said. "You didn't tell me to get the hell away from you, nor did you mention calling security. So I'm asking, is your silence a yes?"

Riley licked her now-dry lips. "My silence? What exactly should I respond 'yes' or 'no' to?"

He didn't actually need to say it. Riley knew what he was asking. She recalled having a similar conversation with him six months ago.

"This isn't new, Riley. It's been brewing between us for years. How long do you plan to keep brushing it off?"

Was that what she'd been doing? Her previous answer to Chaz had been an unequivocal "no." There was nothing between them and to solidify that fact she'd made a point to stay away from him. Which was probably the reason he presumed she'd been running. But tonight, as he'd just stated, she was standing still...and very close to him.

"One night, Riley," he said, his voice going lower.

His face was just inches from hers as he stood in what should have been an uncomfortable stance. But he wasn't trying to move. He just stayed there waiting...for her.

"Give this thing between us one night," he continued.

"There is no 'thing' between us," she whispered.

He eased closer, brushing his lips lightly against hers before pulling back. "Are you sure?"

"Yes."

Chaz stood up straight.

"You're sure there's no 'thing' between us? Or you're sure you won't give us one night?"

"I'm sure you're trying to push my buttons and I'm not in the mood," she replied.

"And yet, you're still standing right here."

"You're in my way," she countered.

Chaz stepped to the side.

"Now I'm not," he said. "And you're still here contemplating whether or not you're up for one night with me. You won't do it. You'll continue to run because that's what suits you."

No. He did not just make this a dare. But as Riley

continued to stare at him, she knew that was exactly what he was doing. Her brothers had done this to her so many times while they were growing up and Riley had never backed down.

But Chaz Warren was not her brother. He was a very attractive man who made her body respond every time she saw him, regardless of what her brain warned. He was the man who had just teased the hell out of her with that chaste kiss. Riley wanted more. She hadn't realized how much until this very moment, but she wanted Chaz Warren in her bed.

"Yes," she said without another thought.

Chaz shook his head and grinned. "You're killing me here, Riley. What exactly are you saying yes to?" he asked.

Tired of this verbal sparring, Riley closed the space between them. She reached up to cup the back of Chaz's head and brought his mouth down to hers for a searing kiss.

CHAPTER THREE

CHAZ HAD NO IDEA. There was no way he could have prepared for how potent the kiss would be. No way in hell.

She looked like any other beautiful woman with hazel eyes and intriguing high cheekbones. Her body was what a teenage boy's wet dreams were made of and she smelled like sin walking. But he'd been around the fashion industry for more than half his life, so none of that was abnormal to him.

Still, the punch in his gut the moment his lips touched hers was nothing to ignore. The warmth that spread slowly to every corner of his body as his tongue brushed against hers and her body pressed closer to his was way beyond what one simple little kiss should have caused.

He'd kissed women before. And had done a whole lot more. But nothing, none of those times, had left him feeling as off balance as he did at this very moment.

With heroic strength Chaz pulled his mouth away from hers. But he did not let her go. He couldn't.

"One night," she said before Chaz had even caught his breath. "In my room. You'll be gone first thing in the morning. And we will never...ever speak of this again."

She was giving him the rules. Chaz was never good at following rules, especially not ones that he hadn't come up with. However, he knew exactly who he was dealing with and what was at stake for both of them if they proceeded.

"I'd rather twenty-four hours, but we can play that by ear. When the time comes, if you still want me to, I'll leave when the sun comes up, but it starts right here, right now," he said before taking her mouth again.

This time it was his tongue pushing her lips apart as he sought the warmth inside. She seemed surprised at first but was clearly ready for their go-round within seconds. Her hands—pressing against the back of his neck as if she thought she was guiding this kiss—felt too good to focus on. There was so much more Chaz wanted to explore with Riley and he only had one night to get it all in.

Her tongue joined his, stroking in a rhythm that seemed practiced and new at the same time. His hands moved down to the dip in her back just before the curve of her ass. Chaz pressed her close to him as he took the kiss deeper. She was tall, probably about five feet seven or eight without the heels she was wearing, so she fit against him perfectly. And with the feel of her body against his, Chaz couldn't wait to get her naked.

Riley moved her hands, slipping them past his shoulders to press firmly against his chest. Chaz immediately pulled back.

"Not here, not like this," she said and looked around as if she thought someone might see them.

They were alone on the balcony, the party inside going full swing without a care for the two people who'd slipped out. But Chaz understood. It was no secret that Riley did not like the press. She did the required press releases and interviews, but she tried to stay out of the spotlight. It didn't matter—her family's company was one of the most talked about in the industry. There was no way the press would stop doing stories on her; even though Riley and Walter Stone hadn't married and the phenomenal partnering of RGold Fashions and Stonemill Apparel, a renowned global distributor, was off, they still covered her and they weren't always kind.

Chaz didn't answer immediately. He kept his arms around her and walked them back until they were standing on the other side of a decorated and lit Christmas tree at the far end of the balcony.

With her back pressed against the wall of the building, Riley still looked up at him with concern.

Chaz touched a finger to her cheek and let it slide slowly down to the line of her jaw.

"I'll protect you, Riley," he said softly. "You don't ever have to worry about that."

"I don't need your protection," she said.

Chaz smiled. "I know," he told her. "But I'll do it, anyway."

He kissed her again, his hands moving down her sides. She wrapped her arms around his neck, holding him tightly against her. Chaz groaned at the spurt of possession and need. He grabbed the hem of her dress, pushing it up her legs so he could feel more of her skin, get even closer to her. Riley dragged one leg up, wrapping it around his waist until he was delightfully trapped in her grasp.

He couldn't believe he was here, with Riley Gold, touching her and kissing her. His erection pulsed and pressed eagerly against his zipper. He wanted to be inside her now, but he couldn't pull himself away from her to get them to the elevators and eventually to her room. He needed something first. He needed to give her something, just this little bit to relax her and to promise himself what was to come.

Chaz moved his hand until he felt the silky skin of her inner thigh. She bucked instantly and tilted her head back to arch into him. He cursed, his mouth sliding over her bared shoulder.

Heat greeted his fingers before he even slipped the thin piece of silk covering her mound to the side. She'd eased her hands inside his jacket and now her nails dug into his chest. He slid two fingers inside her and she gasped. She jerked at the contact, groaning as he pressed deeper and shifted her hips until she could move in rhythm with his thrusts. He gritted his teeth at the delicious feel of her moist heat and the tightness that circled him. Closing his eyes, he clenched his teeth at how good this felt even though it wasn't his hard dick easing in and out of her.

She gripped his shirt in her fists as her body tensed. The sound of his fingers moving in and out of her echoed in his ears and had his dick jumping. She gasped and stilled, her heated walls gripping him tighter before her release came, her body trembled and she moaned in his arms.

Seconds later, fireworks popped off, and the sound of people cheering and singing filtered out from the ballroom onto the balcony.

It had taken them exactly sixteen minutes to weave through the celebrating crowd in the ballroom and head toward the elevators. When they finally arrived at the door to her suite, Riley unlocked it and led Chaz inside. She dropped her purse and the key card on the sofa table and kept moving through the lavishly decorated space. Chaz stopped at the fully stocked bar tucked in a corner of the living room and asked Riley if she wanted champagne. She opted for wine and Chaz selected water. Now they were sitting on the terrace, finishing their drinks and watching the last of the fireworks show.

It didn't take a genius to see that her nerves were more than a little frayed. Probably a combination of the crowd they'd encountered in the hallway and the fact that he was actually in her room. So they would slow down a bit until she was certain of herself and what she wanted from him once more.

"Why are you here alone?" she asked after a few minutes of silence.

Chaz sat back on the lounge chair, his legs spread in front of him.

"I always travel alone."

"Yet you always find someone to spend your time with," she countered.

Chaz looked over to her.

"What?" she asked as he continued to stare. "You're in the papers a lot. With this woman and that woman. Between you, Maurice and Major, I don't know who the true Fashion House Playboy is."

Considering she'd lumped him into a category with two of her brothers, Chaz figured the comment wasn't a total insult.

"For a person burned by the lies in tabloids, you should know better than to believe anything they print," he replied, anyway, but then wondered if he'd gone too far. The last thing he wanted was to irritate her.

"You're right," she countered, quicker than he expected.

"But if you want to know if I have a girlfriend, the answer is no."

Her fingers moved on her thigh, but she didn't speak. They'd slowed down, Chaz thought. From the time they'd first come up here, until now, her fingers had gone from clenching together, to rubbing along the stem of the wineglass, to resting on her thigh. Chaz had never seen Riley nervous. He doubted she felt that way often and he almost smiled with the realization that she must be relaxing with him.

"Do you have a boyfriend?"

Chaz was almost positive she was single, but he didn't want her to think he was presumptuous.

"No," she replied. "I'm not in the market for a boyfriend, fiancé or husband. I'm fine being single."

Because the other way hadn't worked for her. Chaz knew and had no desire to rehash any of that for her.

"So am I," he said.

"Why? Your uncle definitely believes in the institution of marriage. I'm surprised he's not pressuring you to settle down."

"That's precisely why I'm still single," Chaz admitted. "Uncle Tobias was on his fourth wife when he took me in after my parents' deaths. Twenty-four years later and he's on wife number eight. He averages around three to four years with each one, before he decides to trade for a newer model."

"Wow, that's a little harsh. You don't think he's really falling in love with them?"

"Only if he can fall out of love with them just as often. It seems like a vicious cycle to me."

"A cycle indeed," she added. "My parents may be the exception to the rule. They've been married for thirty-eight years this coming June. I think theirs is a real, true love."

"But you're not looking for that yourself?"

She shook her head. "Absolutely not. My focus right now is on RGF. That's all."

"Yes, it's about to get busy on the work front for both of us. But you should always have a balance between work and play," he said and then stood. "Do you want another glass of wine?"

Another drink, more small talk, whatever it took to make Riley feel comfortable with the deal they'd made. He could still smell her sweet and intoxicating scent on his fingers and his erection hadn't abated, but there was no rush. They had all night.

Then what?

Then nothing. They'd get up in the morning and go home. Done.

When she nodded, Chaz took their glasses inside. He poured them both some wine and returned to the terrace. Riley was standing now, too, leaning a hip against the railing as she watched him walk toward her. Chaz handed her the glass.

"Do you have a New Year's resolution?" she asked.

He shrugged. "Never make them. My professional goals are the same each year."

Chaz watched as one of her elegantly arched brows lifted.

"What about your personal goals? Balance of work and play, remember?"

She smiled and Chaz felt the air leave his lungs. Straight white teeth and plump lips. The memory of their scorching kisses would forever be emblazoned on his mind. But it wasn't her mouth that had physically assaulted Chaz in that moment, it was the light he saw flash in her eyes. The little bit of laughter that had joined her smile.

"I want to take more time to paint," he admitted. Something he'd never told anyone else.

"You're an artist?"

"Something like that," he said before downing the contents of his glass. He was suddenly very thirsty.

And very ready to take her. Chaz looked at the empty glass momentarily and then walked over to a table and set it down.

When he returned to stand in front of Riley, he asked, "What's your New Year's resolution?"

She tilted her head as she contemplated a response.

"To have a kick-ass launch at every event this year," she replied without hesitation.

Chaz stepped closer, lifting a hand to cup her cheek. "Then let's not think about work tonight. If this is the only time you'll have for play this year, let's make it count."

He'd been rubbing his thumb over the smooth skin of her cheek when it brushed past her lip. In seconds she was licking the same spot. His cock jumped.

"I agree. We'll make tonight count," she whispered.

Chaz took her glass and set it on the table next to his before pulling her into his arms, taking her mouth into a hot kiss. She returned his kiss with fervor, twining her arms around his neck and pulling him closer.

There wasn't any part of her that he didn't want to touch, kiss, lick and thoroughly enjoy. He couldn't thank her enough for agreeing to this, for wanting this as much as he did. Dragging his mouth from her lips, he suckled her neck, his hands going flat on her back before he unzipped her dress.

"Happy New Year, Riley," he whispered the moment his fingers moved along her bare skin.

She shocked and pleased him immensely by pressing a hand between their bodies and finding his rigid erection before unzipping his pants. "Happy New Year, Chaz."

CHAPTER FOUR

HE WAS HARD and hot in her hands. When her slim fingers wrapped around his thick cock, Riley sighed with pleasure, while the persistent hum of arousal grew in the pit of her stomach. After unzipping his pants and freeing his erection, she'd closed her eyes to savor the feel of him and the wonder of this moment. She was actually doing this, and she was enjoying it.

Opening her eyes, Riley glanced down to see her hands on him. Their skin tones were different, hers lighter, his darker. Her fingers seemed too small against his length and width, yet she jerked him slowly, sliding her fingers from the base of his cock until her thumb brushed over the tip.

Chaz sucked in a breath and groaned, "Do that again."

She did, but not because he said so, because she liked it, too. His skin felt silky and the sound of his groan rubbed along the most primal part of her. The part that enjoyed the power she had at this moment.

"I thought about…this." She'd almost admitted that she'd thought about him specifically instead of simply fantasizing about the physical that was now happening. For Riley there was a distinct difference—thinking about him on a personal level could include wondering what his hobbies were, his favorite meal or movie, while considering how it would feel to kiss him or have sex with him was physical, pure and simple.

"You thought about jerking me off until I came in your hands." His voice was low but deep.

Her fingers stilled over his tip, feeling the first drops of warm moisture.

"I thought about you, too, Riley. I thought about taking your mouth in a hot-as-hell kiss." As if to punctuate that statement he cupped her cheeks and pressed his lips to hers. The kiss was chaste for only a second, before his tongue pushed through the barrier of her lips, tangling instantly with hers until she was breathless.

"I thought about getting my hands on you," he continued when his mouth was moving over the soft skin of her jaw.

Riley continued stroking him while tilting her neck back so he could have better access. Just a few minutes ago they'd toasted the New Year, now Riley felt as if she needed another drink. Anything to cool the heat that was soaring through her at this moment.

"Harder, Riley, honey. Stroke me harder."

He was pumping into her hand as his tongue trailed a hot path down her skin.

"Yeah, like that," he groaned and nipped the skin of her collarbone with his teeth.

Riley shivered and clenched her teeth as she fought to hold in the moan of pleasure that soared through her body. This was just sex. It wasn't some epiphany that would change the way she viewed relationships or even how she felt about Chaz and his family.

She needed his clothes off and moved her hands from his rigid length up to his chest, where she was about to push his jacket over his shoulders. A loud sound stopped her and Riley realized it was more fireworks popping off. She looked around them quickly and felt a cool breeze over her bare skin.

Damn! They were still outside on the balcony. Riley backed away from him, praying no one had seen them. Chaz's gaze found hers, and before she could speak he scooped her up, carrying her through the glass doors and into the bedroom.

While he took his time laying her down on the bed, his hands moved furiously to remove her dress. Riley was just about to lift her leg to remove her shoe when he said, "Leave them."

She shivered, this time from a chill and the way he was staring at her with such raw hunger. For a moment Riley thought she might have gone too far. Was she really going to do this? It had been so long... too long.

"Everybody thinks you're perfect. They have no idea." He sounded as if he were in awe, his voice running like warm oil along every nerve in her body.

She propped herself up on her elbows and dragged her legs onto the bed slowly until the spiked heel of her shoe dug into the cream-colored silk duvet. With her eyes locked on his, Riley let her knees fall apart and reveled in the quick hiss of breath he expelled before the guttural curse that followed.

If nothing else, Chaz Warren was damn good for her ego.

He looked at her as if she were the only woman in the world—no, as if she were the only woman in the world *he* wanted. That want was apparent in his eyes, which had grown darker than their usual russet-brown color. His lips thinned as his tongue snaked out to ease over them. He looked hungry and she felt as if she were sitting on a sterling-silver tray, offering herself to him.

Chaz snatched his jacket off. His fingers moved lightning fast over the bow tie and buttons of his shirt, until his chest was bare and it was Riley's turn to lick her lips at the delectable specimen standing before her.

"I've watched you for so long, wondering what this moment would finally feel like."

Why did his voice arouse her this way? He was just a man talking as men sometimes did during sex. It should not have sent shivers down her spine or caused her thighs to tremble. But it did.

She'd already undone the buckle of his pants so all he had to do was push them and his boxers down his toned legs. He paused to remove his wallet from his back pocket.

He pulled out a strip of condoms and tossed them onto the bed beside her. "I don't know if this is gonna be enough for twenty-four hours."

"I have some," she told him before reaching for the plastic and ripping one packet from the others.

While he finished removing his pants, boxers and shoes, Riley tore open the condom packet and tossed the plastic to the side. She was just about to sit up so that she could put the condom on him, when Chaz stood at the end of the bed. Her fingers paused over the latex while she soaked in every gorgeous inch of his body. In the dimness of the room—there was only light from the small lamp near the window she'd forgotten to turn off when she left—he looked like a chocolate Adonis. Every part of his body was perfectly sculpted, from the bulging biceps and pectoral muscles to his tapered waist and beautiful erection, which jutted forward as if it, too, were glad this moment had finally arrived. But even with all that, Riley's eyes went right back to his shoulders. She definitely had a thing for good strong shoulders on a man.

"Tonight, you can have whatever you want, Riley."

Like he could read her mind, Chaz reached out to take one of her ankles in his hand. She had no idea what he was about to do but didn't really give a damn as long as he buried his long cock deep inside her as soon as humanly possible.

Chaz lifted that leg until it was extended straight into the air. He kissed her ankle and rubbed his hand up her bare calf. The closer his fingers came to her inner thigh, Riley's fingers trembled and she almost dropped the condom she'd forgotten she was holding. He inched higher until his fingers touched the tender folds of her pussy, easing through them to find that she was already slick with need.

"Is this for me?" he asked, and Riley had to gulp hard before she could form a coherent response.

"Tonight," she whispered.

For a moment Chaz looked as if he wanted to say something else, but he nodded instead. He dragged two fingers down her slit, back and forth until the sound of her arousal mixing with the motion echoed in the room. She gasped because a single touch had never made her this edgy and needy before. Riley wanted to jump up and wrap her legs around him. She wanted him inside her. Now!

With that thought, she rose and reached for him. Chaz was faster. He grasped her wrists, stopping her from touching him.

"We don't have to rush," he said. "I want to take my time with you, Riley. I want you to remember every second of this night."

Riley shook her head. "I want it now. Hot and fast."

He did not immediately respond and in those quiet seconds Riley realized she ached enough to beg. But, oh, how she prayed she wouldn't have to. Every higher deity in the universe must have heard her prayer because in the next seconds Chaz slipped the condom from her fingers and sheathed his thick length. He pushed her back onto the bed and lifted both her ankles to rest on his shoulders.

"This time," he said, his brow furrowed as he eased onto the bed. "Just this one time we'll go fast."

Riley didn't know if she should thank him or not, but the thought died when Chaz planted his hands under her ass cheeks and spread her enough so that his dick could slide into her with one slow and viciously erotic thrust.

Chaz knew exactly what was happening here. He should have guessed it would go this way. Riley would fight to control every situation. She would hold on to that control like a safety net and the only way beneath the shields she'd erected around not just her heart, but her entire life, was through pleasure. It was the one thing she couldn't fight, because she hadn't received enough of it in her life. She hungered for it even though she would never allow herself to admit that. But Chaz knew and he'd waited long enough for the moment where he could start to push past her barriers.

He'd eased into her until his heavy sac touched the

warm wetness of her folds. She'd stretched for him so beautifully, her walls opening and then gripping him so tight he'd had to close his eyes to the staggering bliss. His entire body had gone still as his mind wrapped itself around the feel of her.

Now Chaz pulled out until only the tip remained sheathed by her heat. He watched her arms slam down onto the bed, fingers gathering the duvet as she squeezed, and shook her head. "Don't," she whimpered.

"Shh. I got you," he promised and slammed into her again.

She wanted fast and hot. Chaz would oblige.

His knees were on the bed now and he grasped her ankles again, spreading her legs this time until they were in a wide V. He thrust into her in quick succession, watching as every emotion from surprise to fulfillment flitted across her face. Her hair had been so neat he'd been afraid to touch it while in the ballroom, but now strands had broken free of the smooth knot, falling around her face in an angelic fashion.

"Yes!" Her teeth were clenched as the word fell from her lips. Her eyes were closed, full breasts moving with each thrust.

Chaz moved a hand down until his thumb covered her clit. She gasped and he smiled on the inside.

"This hot enough for you?" He circled her clit with the gentlest touch.

She panted and nodded.

"Look at me, Riley." Chaz didn't want her to just remember every second of this night. He wanted her to remember everything he did to her. Every touch, kiss and spark of pleasure he elicited from her.

Her eyes opened slowly as if she were waking from a deep slumber—lovely cognac-brown eyes with just a hint of red along the edges. How many times had Chaz awakened in the middle of the night, dick hard and on the brink of embarrassing the hell out of himself, because those eyes had taunted him in his dreams? Too damn many.

He pulled his hand back and slipped a finger slowly into his mouth, his dick throbbing inside her as her intent gaze followed that finger from his lips and back down. He touched her clit again and she closed her eyes.

"No, Riley. Open those pretty eyes, baby. I want you to see everything I do to you."

Her eyes popped open quickly and Chaz circled her clit with his damp finger while only marginally slowing his thrusts into her. She yanked a hand away from the blanket to reach up and cup her breast. Squeezing so her pebble-hard nipple peeked between her fingers. Chaz clenched his teeth at the sexy sight.

"Tell me you want it faster, Riley. Tell me now!"

She was moaning and stroking her breast. "Faster!" It was an emphatic whimper and Chaz loved the sound.

He pounded into her, continuing to work her clit until she was gasping and moaning. He wanted to hear her say his name but knew she wouldn't. Not without him prompting her. And Chaz wasn't going to prompt her. Not for everything. There were pieces of Riley he wanted, but only if she gave them freely. And right now, all she was about to give him was her release.

"Fast and hot," he groaned. "You're so fuckin' hot, Riley! I don't care what anybody else says, you're scorching hot, baby!"

She arched off the bed, her thighs trembling as her release stormed through her body.

"Yes! Give it all to me, Riley! Give me what's mine."

Chaz lost himself in the moment. Glorious sensations rippling over every muscle in his body as he continued moving in and out of her. There'd never been a place that felt like this. The perfect fit, the deep thrusts, the mind-boggling feeling that pulsed through him as he gritted his teeth and held on tightly to her ankles when his own release filled the condom.

When he could take a breath without feeling as if he were going to pass out, Chaz kissed both her ankles and smiled at those sexy-as-hell heels she was still wearing. He was just about to ease her legs down to the bed, pull out of her and lie beside her, when Riley moved first.

She lowered her legs, ignoring his grip that instantly loosened. She was away from him and off the bed in seconds. Chaz was still on his knees blinking as she grabbed a black silk robe from a chair and carried it into the bathroom, where she immediately closed and locked the door.

CHAPTER FIVE

Okay, that was done.

It was good. Damn good.

But it was done.

So why were her thighs still trembling and her body already missing the warmth of his?

Riley kicked off her shoes, dropped her robe onto the closed toilet and rested her palms on the cool marble top of the sink. She lowered her head and took a deep breath. When she looked up, the woman staring back at her through the mirror was only slightly foreign. Her eyes were bright with remnants of desire. Her cheeks were flushed, lips plump from his kisses. Delicious kisses that had served as the appetizer to a greater entrée she couldn't have imagined if she'd tried.

She wanted him again. *Dammit!*

Riley turned on the water, hoping the noise would take the foolish thoughts from her mind, but then realized they'd agreed to twenty-four hours or at the very least sunrise tomorrow. He'd only been there an hour and a half, which meant she still had plenty of time to indulge in Chaz's scrumptious body. She leaned forward and splashed water on her face. It was cool and her body shivered with the contact. She pulled her hair free from the pins that still partially held it back and took the next few minutes to wash up.

She'd intended to take some time to clean up and then return to the bedroom, to face the music so to speak. Instead Riley pushed her arms into the sleeves of her robe and tied it tightly around her waist before moving to sit on the lip of the soaker tub, and closed her eyes.

She'd had sex with Chaz Warren.

And not one time had he complained about her not making enough noise, or not praising every move he made. There'd been no requests for her to do anything he'd read about online or saw in some movie. She wasn't given instructions on how to please him and she'd never once had to wonder if he would please her. Riley's orgasm had come like a full-blown explosion of sensation that still had her body quaking.

Walt had always complained. Nothing Riley did was ever right for him, and to be honest, she'd stopped trying long before she'd caught her ex with another woman.

I won't go into specifics but things could get pretty frigid in Riley's bedroom.

Riley closed her eyes as she recalled the quote she'd read in the newspaper the day after she'd walked calmly out of Walt's condo, leaving him and a model she'd seen before—but would love to never see again—naked in bed. She hated that she remembered those words and hated more how they still made her angry. She wouldn't allow them to make her self-conscious. Riley knew how to bring herself pleasure and she'd had a few experiences with other men besides Walt, so she knew his words had been laced with vindictiveness. If their sex life wasn't what it should have been, Riley wasn't solely to blame. But she'd wanted to spare her family and the reputation of their company so no rebuttal to Walt's inappropriate declaration was made.

Which was why this fling between her and Chaz would definitely end in twenty-four hours. There was no doubt in her mind about that.

With her shoes in hand, Riley walked out of the bathroom and into the empty bedroom. Chaz was gone, and a quick punch of disappointment landed in the pit of her stomach. She walked to the closet and placed her shoes inside before turning slowly to look around once more, confirming that the room was empty.

"I thought you might be thirsty."

She startled at the sound of his voice and glanced in the direction of the door to see Chaz standing there with two glasses of champagne. He was wearing his boxers and nothing else and her body instantly responded with disappointment shifting to the slow burn of arousal.

"Yes. Thank you." For lack of anything better to say, Riley met him as he came into the room and accepted a glass. Her bare feet moved across the plush beige carpet until she could sit on the side of the bed.

"You don't have to be nervous," he said.

She finished the sip of champagne and looked toward the end of the bed where Chaz now sat.

"Why would you think I'm nervous?"

"You're not talking."

"I was drinking."

He shrugged and took a gulp of champagne. "Guess what I mean is that this doesn't have to be uncomfortable. We can just take things as they come."

"Right. For the next twenty-four hours." Riley glanced at the clock. It was almost two in the morning. "I've had a really long day."

"Me, too." Chaz finished his champagne and walked around to the other side of the bed. "I was hoping you weren't going to expect sex all night long. I mean, not that I wouldn't be glad to oblige. I'm pretty sure I wouldn't fall asleep on you. But it might be a good idea to get some rest."

She hadn't meant to, but Riley smiled. "I wasn't expecting sex all night long."

"Great. We agree." He proceeded to arrange the pillows before pulling back the duvet and sheet.

Riley had been watching over her shoulder and set her glass on the nightstand before easing off the bed to pull the bedcovers down on her side. She normally slept in a nightgown but she wasn't about to walk across the room to the bureau where she'd put her clothes to retrieve one. The robe would do just fine for tonight. Her pillows didn't require a lot of adjustment and she lay easily on her side of the bed.

Chaz lay on his side. He pulled the covers midway up his chest. The chest that was still bare and undeniably enticing. There was a scar beneath his left pectoral. She'd seen it when he was standing in the doorway. She wondered how he'd gotten it.

"This is the only time I'm a fan of lights-out in the bedroom." It was an easy comment made seconds before he leaned over and hit the button that turned off both bedside lamps simultaneously.

The room went dark and Riley's heart began to pound a different rhythm. It wasn't a totally unfamiliar feeling but one that she didn't welcome now. She pulled the covers up, tucking them tight beneath her armpits, and closed her eyes. She could do this. She could sleep in the same bed with a guy. Although she'd never done it before.

Riley Eliza Gold was twenty-nine years old, one of the youngest woman executives at RGold Fashions. She'd graduated summa cum laude with a degree in statistics from Columbia and went on to hone her skills at the Parsons School in New York. She was in charge of a multimillion-dollar line within her family's company, their legacy. There was nothing she couldn't do.

Except, at the moment, she was having a hard time regulating her breathing knowing that if she just extended her arm she would touch a man. Chaz Warren, the renowned brand manager for King Designs, her family's biggest rival, to be exact.

That last thought probably wasn't the smartest one she'd had tonight since it only increased her breathing and had her clenching the sheets.

Riley was counting down from one hundred when something moved beneath the sheet. It could have been her imagination since her mind was going at a rapid pace, but no, it wasn't. His foot touched hers and she jumped.

"Shh. It's just me."

Well, of course it was him, who else would be in her bed?

Riley's eyes were wide-open and staring into the darkness. And this was the second time he'd *shh'd* her. She wasn't a child and she didn't like it.

"I figured you weren't the cuddling type, but I wanted to reassure you that you weren't alone." Did his voice sound richer, huskier in the dark?

"I'm definitely not the cuddling type." It was an honest reply even if she didn't exactly like how it sounded. "And I know I'm not alone." Because when she was alone at night she could breathe. She could also fret that she might well be alone forever, but at least she could breathe easily while doing so.

"Do you normally cuddle the women you sleep with?"

"Whoa, I have a strict rule about no discussion of prior lovers while in bed with the current lover."

"We're not lovers." Her response was quick.

He moved over, not close enough to touch her, but close enough that she no longer had to stretch out her arm to touch him.

"For the next twenty-four hours we are."

His feet brushed against hers again, but she didn't jump this time.

"I've cuddled before. I can see the appeal, but it's not high on my list of things to do after sex." He paused. "What about you?"

Riley had already realized the folly in asking that question and she'd hoped he would stick to his rule about not discussing former lovers.

"I don't see the appeal, either." There, she didn't have to admit that Walt was always in a hurry to leave the bed when they were finished, and that with the couple of men she'd slept with in the three years since her very public breakup, she'd been the one to get up and leave first. Just as she'd done with Chaz.

"So we won't cuddle," he said. "We'll just lie here and go to sleep."

"And play footsie?" Riley added.

"Well, since you asked." Chaz turned on his side

and extended his legs so that both of his feet tangled between hers.

They were warm, and focusing so much on this simple yet very different touch had managed to calm the anxiety that was steadily building inside of her. She smiled into the darkness.

Chaz listened as Riley's breathing steadied and she finally fell asleep. He couldn't see the clock but he'd guess maybe a half hour to forty minutes had passed since they'd first climbed into bed. Riley Gold wasn't used to sleeping with men. The assessment kind of went with the tabloid's perception of her, but a part of Chaz had always envisioned her as the intelligent businesswoman who shed that shield in the privacy of her own home, opening up to the man in her life. However, instinct had told him cuddling wasn't on her agenda. That and the fact that she'd gotten into bed and lain so close to the edge he was afraid she might fall off. Still, just as pleasure was the key to tearing down her defenses, touch was one of the first steps to that pleasure.

Their feet were still entwined as she lay on her back and he on his side. She hadn't made any move to get closer to him, but she hadn't ordered him back to his side of the bed, either. That was progress.

Why he was even the least bit concerned about that progress, Chaz had no idea.

This was just sex. Long overdue and really good

sex, but just sex nonetheless. He wasn't in the market for anything else. And neither was she. They were the perfect couple, or noncouple, as their business lives came first.

Except for tonight. Chaz wasn't going to think about his business or the work he was doing for his uncle and he didn't want Riley thinking about her job, either. These moments were reserved for them. While this hadn't been the way Chaz thought he would end his evening, he was glad things had turned in his favor.

He'd had sex with the infamous Riley Gold. A triumphant smile touched his lips but fell away the moment he recalled how quickly she'd jumped up from the bed and run into the bathroom. For a few startled seconds he'd wondered what that was about, but realized he already knew. While the fashion industry might look at Riley like some worldly princess trying to make a name for herself, Chaz had always felt he knew her better. It was strange, this insight into a woman who'd done nothing but brush him off since the first day they'd met.

Chaz wasn't Riley's type—he was too outgoing, had too many women and was too public with his social media background in comparison to the privacy she fought like hell to maintain. And yet, they'd been drawn to each other from the start. So much so that he was barely restraining himself from touching her again. Sure, his feet were on hers and for the last little while he'd been content with that. Now, not so much.

He eased over slightly until the warmth from her body beneath the covers reached out to him. With the lightest touch imaginable, Chaz let his fingers trace a line from her wrist up her bare arm. To do this he'd had to push up the sleeve of her robe. Her skin was so soft and warm he ached to kiss her right there, in the spot where her elbow bent and around to her shoulder, over her back, down to her… She stirred and in the next seconds Chaz knew she was wide-awake. But she'd made no move to push him away.

Chaz eased his hand around her waist and untied the belt of her robe. He pushed the silky material off her arm and pressed his lips lightly to her shoulder. She didn't move or speak but he felt her body relax. He kissed her there again and moved closer to her, so close the hard length of his cock now rubbed against her upper thigh. If she had a reaction to feeling him so hot and ready for her, she wasn't showing it. Despite that little chink in his ego, Chaz continued.

He ran his hand over the parts of her skin he'd just kissed, easing her onto her side so his lips could glide over the skin of her back. Untangling the lower part of his legs from hers allowed Chaz more range to continue tasting her golden skin. The faint hint of her floral perfume lingered and he wondered if she'd rubbed the fragrance over every part of her body. He kissed down the path of her spine, his fingers moving over her skin softly. The small of her back was a delectable little spot where Chaz couldn't help but plant openmouthed kisses, circling his tongue from one side to the other, as if the very act was somehow branding her as his.

She sighed, a quiet little whoosh of breath that encouraged and further aroused him. He planted his palms on the smooth globes of her ass and closed his eyes to sensations rippling through his body at that simple touch. Riley Gold had a great ass. Plump enough to make his dick hard just from watching her walk across the room and delicious enough naked to make him grit his teeth and pray for patience. He'd already given her hot and fast at her request, now Chaz was aiming for nice and slow.

He kissed one rounded half and then the other before touching his tongue lightly to the top of her crease. Her breath quickened but she did not speak. Her body felt relaxed and compliant while the thought of her waiting for what he planned to do next had to be one of the most erotic moments he'd ever experienced.

Chaz didn't keep her guessing. He followed the line with his tongue, gripping her cheeks in his hands until they were overflowing his fingers. When he was down far enough, he extended his tongue until he could touch the warm lips of her pussy. She was already wet for him. He groaned and took another lick.

"I love that you're already bare for me." He murmured the words and didn't know if she heard them or not before his tongue was on her heated flesh once more.

He slid his hand from her bottom to her thigh and lifted her top leg higher, giving himself greater access. His mouth was fully open now and all over her with slow but hungry strokes of his tongue. It was a cliché but Chaz didn't give a damn, she tasted so irresistibly sweet. He never wanted to stop tasting her. But her thighs had already begun to shake and his dick was painfully hard, poking through the slit in his boxers. He was going to pull away and grab a condom, in just a second, after he licked her right there...

Riley hissed loudly and arched her back the second his tongue inched inside her warm entrance. She shattered in his hands, her moans echoing in the room while her climax shook her body.

Chaz moved the moment she was still again. He rolled over to the side of the bed where he'd left his empty champagne glass and the strip of condoms. He pulled one free, tore open the packet and sheathed his bobbing length. When he eased onto the bed again, he reached around to touch Riley's chin, turning her face toward his.

"Tonight, it's only about pleasure, Riley. Yours. Mine. Nothing or nobody else. Understand?"

He could feel that she was nodding but Chaz needed to hear the words. He wanted to hear her voice.

"Say it. Tell me you want this. That you want me. Say it, Riley."

He hadn't realized how desperately he needed to hear those words. The feeling was urgent and deeply seated inside him, just as the need to break down her barriers was. Chaz couldn't explain either circumstance. He wasn't in the market for a girlfriend or any type of commitment. Sure, he'd wanted Riley in his bed for a long time, but this was different. He knew it even though he couldn't explain it.

"I want you." Her voice was husky and sexier than any other sound he'd ever heard. "I want this." She reached up to flatten her palms on his chest and moved them slowly down until she could wrap her fingers around his thick length. "I want it all right now, Chaz. Right. Now."

She was still lying on her side but had turned slightly to touch him. Chaz touched her hip and then reluctantly eased her hand away from his length. It was a necessary bit of torture so that he could completely remove her robe. When that was done, he returned her to the position on her side, with her plump ass facing him.

"You can have it now," he whispered and lifted her top leg so that he could slide between her thighs. "You can have anything, Riley. Any damn thing you want." He clenched his teeth as he slid deep into her with one long stroke. He was buried inside, and still, Chaz felt the burning desire for more. He began stroking in and out, loving the feel of her heated moisture gliding seamlessly along his rigid dick. He closed his eyes and let the pleasure overtake him while one word echoed in his mind repeatedly: *damn*.

In one night, Riley Gold might have completely damned him.

CHAPTER SIX

"LET'S GO SIGHTSEEING," Chaz suggested the next morning. "Isn't that what people do in Milan?"

They were sitting across from each other at a round table positioned close to a window.

"Unless you're in the industry and then Milan's mostly about work." Her response was a bit curt as she stared down at her tablet. She moved a finger over the screen, going from one email message to another, reading and scribbling notes in the stripe-covered notebook beside the tablet. To the other side was a small plate with an untouched croissant and a half-full cup of coffee that was undoubtedly cold by now.

"You do know what a vacation is, don't you, Riley?" He didn't wait for her to respond. "It's when you leave work at the office and just relax. Lie in bed all day or go see places you normally don't get a chance to see when you're so busy working."

She didn't move her head but raised her eyes to stare at him. It was one of the sexiest things he'd ever seen.

"I know what a vacation is. I also know that Fashion Week is right around the corner—"

"And it'll still be around the corner when we return to New York tomorrow."

She shook her head and returned to her emails. "I'm not surprised you don't understand."

"What's that supposed to mean?" Chaz was sitting back in the chair, his tuxedo pants on but not buttoned, his feet and chest bare.

Riley sighed and crossed one leg over the other. "You're not as invested in this business as I am. Sure, you're at King Designs now, rebranding all of Tobias's lines that are flailing, but everybody knows your real love is your social media chain."

She knew more about him than Chaz had presumed. He'd process how he felt about that later. Right now, Ms. Gold needed to be corrected.

"I don't do anything half-assed," he countered.

"That's not what I meant."

"But it's how you presented it. And yeah, I came back to New York to help my uncle rebrand some of the lines that had taken a backseat to the expensive couture designs. I'm rebuilding areas that needed more attention not because they're flailing, but because King Designs needs to remain a full-service fashion house. And thankfully, Conversation Media, my Fortune 500 company, is doing well enough that I could afford to step away for a while to do what I can for family. That's called loyalty."

She tilted her head and folded her arms over her chest. She'd gotten out of the bed before him, and when he woke, she was wearing fuchsia satin pajama pants and top. Her hair had been smoothed back and hung in a long tail down her back. She wasn't wearing any makeup and was still stunning.

"Again, I didn't mean to offend you. I was just saying that you may not have as much at stake since King is your secondary job."

He wondered if she realized she'd just offended him again. Luckily, Chaz had a thick skin and was more amused than offended. Riley honestly thought she was stating a fact and nothing else.

"My family is important to me. Just as yours is to you. But putting that aside, this is still a vacation. So, let's get dressed and head out for a fun-filled day like other coup—ah, other tourists."

With any other woman Chaz might have been lucky enough to avoid the mistake he'd just made. Not with Riley.

"We are not a couple. And for that reason, plus a half dozen others, we cannot go traipsing around Milan seeing the sights and soaking up the local flavor."

"The couple thing is just a title. Tell me the real reason you don't want to go out." Because she was being way too adamant about this.

"That's the reason. We're not a couple. In fact, for all intents and purposes, we're enemies. The press would have a ball writing headlines about us being together in Milan and my father would freak when he saw them. Your uncle probably would, too."

"That feud is theirs not ours." He knew that wasn't going to be enough so he held up a hand to stop her rebuttal. "But I get it. Why add fuel to the flame? Fine. Then we'll have to figure out something fun we can do in this room."

Riley arched one elegant brow and Chaz's dick jumped on command.

"Man, Riley, you are killing me!" he groaned and shook his head. "But I'd rather not spend my one and only day with *the* Riley Gold in bed. And if you ever repeat that I'll have to kill you."

She laughed.

It was a quick burst that sounded so pure and so infectious that Chaz found himself smiling, too.

"So tell me, if I wasn't here right now and you weren't working, what would you do today?"

She was still smiling when she shrugged. "Probably lie on the couch and watch movies."

"Okay." He shook his head. "We can do that. What type of movies do you like?"

He almost said he didn't want to watch any romantic comedies or movies where women got even by killing their spouses or whoever wronged them, but he refrained. If she named a movie like that Chaz would have to suck it up and watch, just for the sake of being with her.

"You sure you want me to pick the movie?"

No. He wasn't.

"Yeah, I'm sure."

"Okay, but don't forget this was your idea."

It *wasn't* cozy sitting on the hotel couch with her legs stretched over Chaz's lap. And she *hadn't* enjoyed the risotto alla Milanese much more than she had ever before because he'd been laughing at her for eating what was essentially a bowl of rice while he savored his so-called heartier dish of osso buco.

Similarly, the movie they were watching was one of her favorites. She'd seen it so many times that she'd saved it on her tablet, which they'd hooked up to the television. So the reason she was laughing and seeing Joe and Kathleen fall in love differently had nothing to do with Chaz's lively commentary throughout the film. Nothing at all.

And she absolutely was not turned on by the fact that he'd watched not only one of her favorite romantic comedies, but three. They were on their fourth one. They'd been on this couch all day, getting up only to use the bathroom and answer the door for room service. Riley couldn't recall when she'd spent such a relaxing and entertaining day. But she wasn't going to give Chaz all the credit. He just happened to be here with her. All day long.

With that thought Riley pulled her legs away from

his lap, bringing them up to her chest, and wrapped her arms around them.

"We can turn this off now. It's almost over, anyway," she told him.

He'd watched her legs as they moved and now dragged those sinfully dark brown eyes up to meet hers.

"When it's over, we can pick the next one or go sit on the balcony for a while if you need to get some air."

Riley needed more than air to understand why she'd put herself in this position in the first place. It was foolish to believe she could spend one full day with this man, or any man for that matter. Why bother kidding herself about ever having a fulfilling relationship? That wasn't in the plans.

"I think I've watched enough movies for today."

Riley stared at the television. She'd seen enough women find their perfect guys and keep them. Yes, watching romantic comedies with him was an even bigger mistake than agreeing to this twenty-four-hour tryst.

"Is that really what's going on, Riley?"

Her head snapped back so she could look at him. "I know when I've had enough of watching movies, Chaz."

This was the second time today she'd snapped at him. The first had been during breakfast when he'd done exactly what he was doing now—looking at her as if he knew something she was too daft or too stubborn to admit.

"Or have you had enough of this?"

This?

It was nothing. That was what she'd been telling herself for the past few hours when her mind drifted to how their current situation resembled so many of the movies they'd been watching. A man and a woman getting to know each other, feeling the attraction between them brewing and deciding how best to proceed to get what they wanted most—happy-ever-after.

"I agreed to one night and then went along with a full twenty-four hours," she said because that was the best excuse she had for getting herself into this predicament. Riley did not go back on her word, no matter how uncomfortable she might feel.

"And you were fine with that twenty-four hours being just about sex."

"That's all there is," she replied and turned on the couch to drop her legs to the floor. The former position made her feel too vulnerable, to unsure of herself.

"That's cool, Riley. If you can't take anything else, we can do what we agreed."

Chaz got up from the couch and came to stand in front of her.

"Here or in the bedroom?"

After breakfast he'd gone down to his room. When he returned, he was wearing sweatpants, pristine white tennis shoes and a white T-shirt that molded to every indentation of his chest. All of that gorgeousness was standing in front of her now, offering her everything she'd dreamed of sexually. Riley swallowed. Hard.

From this position it was just a matter of reaching out, pushing the pants down past his hips and freeing his cock. She could have him in her mouth in seconds. She'd thought about that very act all night long.

"I wouldn't have guessed this arrangement would irritate you so much. After all, it was your suggestion." Her words were a stall tactic, which Riley hated having to use.

"Not irritated, Riley, baby. Aroused."

He licked his lips and lifted a hand to his chest, letting it glide slowly down until it grazed the very noticeable and very hard bulge of his dick through the sweatpants.

She resisted the urge to lick her lips, too.

"I know the difference, Chaz. And regardless of our agreement, I'm not going to have angry sex with you."

He tossed his head back and laughed.

"You're not going to watch movies with me all day long and you're not going to have sex with me. So, tell me, Riley, what are we going to do?"

This was ridiculous. It was frustrating and embarrassing. All the things she'd felt anytime she was with Walt.

"Fine," she snapped.

Her fingers shook only slightly as she grabbed the waist of his sweatpants. He took another step closer and Riley pushed the pants down past his hips. She didn't bother pushing the boxers down, but instead reached her hand inside the opening and grabbed his dick.

"That's it, baby. Take what you want."

His words were raspy and sounded dirty.

She liked them.

Riley scooted her butt to the edge of the couch, spreading her legs so that Chaz was now standing between them. She jerked her hand from the base of his length to the tip, watching hungrily as her fingers moved over the silky dark skin. Her mouth watered and she dipped her head, extended her tongue and took her first taste.

She owned a penthouse in Manhattan, a Lamborghini, had a trust fund she hadn't touched a penny of yet and, thanks to her budding career and smart investments, became a millionaire years ago at the age of twenty-five. But nothing she'd accomplished up to this point in her life had given Riley the surge of power she felt with Chaz's dick in her mouth.

With her throat muscles relaxed, she took in his full length. Hollowing her cheeks, she sucked while her tongue licked the bottom of his shaft. One hand was still at the base of his dick, holding him in place while the other fondled his heavy sac. Her eyes were closed as she worked her mouth over him while the sound of his guttural moans and the feel of his fingers raking over her scalp, pushing away the band that held her hair, rang like music to her ears.

He pulled back and pumped into her mouth with slow movements that almost seemed painful if the sound of his grunts were any indication. But the way he held her head so tight to him and the slight tremble in his thighs when she held him deep in her throat made Riley feel as if she were flying. Soaring actually, over the entire world that had read Walt's stupid article and believed every word about her being frigid and inexperienced in the bedroom.

"Damn! Your freakin' mouth!" His words were punctuated with deep breaths and loud exhales. "Your sweet, hot little mouth."

Riley let her lips slide over his dick as she pulled back slowly. He wrapped her hair around his fingers and gripped tighter, trying to keep her from releasing him completely. That wasn't her plan. Instead she flicked her tongue over the crest of his cock, easing into the slit that dripped sugared drops of his precum. He hissed, sucking air through clenched teeth as his head fell back on his shoulders. Riley had looked up just in time to see the moment of surrender in this infamous sophisticated billionaire. Triumph was like a nightcap and they hadn't even experienced the full meal yet.

She knew the moment Chaz had reached his breaking point when just as she sucked him in deep again and tightened her mouth around him, he released her head and stepped back from her hastily.

"Take off your clothes," he grumbled as he pulled his shirt up and over his head in a matter of seconds.

Riley didn't bother being offended by his command. She could still be in control of this interlude. When she was naked, she stood. Chaz had just finished removing his shoes and was taking a condom out of his wallet before tossing the wallet onto the table and pushing his pants and boxers down and off. He must have replenished his condom stash when he went to his room because the two leftover from last night were still on the nightstand in the bedroom. This one Chaz held between his teeth while he removed the rest of his clothes. Riley stepped forward, snapping the packet away from him. She tore it open and removed the latex so that when he stood gloriously naked in front of her she quickly sheathed him.

"This is what you want?" It was a question he didn't give her a chance to answer because before Riley could speak Chaz wrapped an arm around her waist and pulled her against his chest.

She tilted her head to stare up at him and he bent down to meet her, crashing his lips over hers and taking a brutally hot kiss. Tongues, teeth and moans mixed and mingled while naked bodies pressed together in the middle of the living room in a luxury Milan hotel. This could have been a scene in a movie— a tawdry sex flick, not the romantic comedies they'd been watching all day.

He lifted her off the floor, wrapping her legs around his waist while his mouth still worked over hers. Riley wrapped her arms tightly around his neck as Chaz moved them back to the couch. She wasn't thinking of anything now besides how good his kisses were and how the taste of him would forever be emblazoned in her mind when he sat on the couch, holding her close on his lap. Riley eagerly pulled away from his mouth. She dropped her hands between their bodies and grabbed his cock while lifting her body to position herself over him.

"Now." She breathed the single word just as the tip of his dick touched her wet opening.

"Whatever you want," he replied before taking her nipple between his teeth for a quick tug.

Riley gasped and slammed down onto him. He filled her completely, snugly but comfortably. It took her a couple seconds to let the pleasure of his presence inside ripple up her spine and spread throughout her body. Then she was riding, coming up on her knees and rotating her hips in a rhythm that once again had Chaz gasping and murmuring something about her lips, her tightness and how much he enjoyed all of the above. She marveled in the words, let them wash over her along with the unmitigated pleasure sex with him was bringing her. He matched her rhythm, cupping her butt tightly and licking her breasts as she arched over him.

Riley was definitely soaring now, but this time it was over puffy white clouds that lulled her into a place where only pleasure existed. She bounced over him knowing that it could only get better from this point.

"Yes, Riley! Take everything you want. Let go and take it all."

He gave her permission. She took it and more until her release crashed over her, splintering her into a million pieces that scattered over sweet blissful clouds.

CHAPTER SEVEN

Manhattan, New York
One week later

RILEY WAS IN her element. She walked around her desk, flipping through the report that Korey, her assistant, had just handed her.

"These projections are off." She glanced across the page to the end of each row, then down to the bottom to get the totals. Numbers were Riley's nirvana. She'd always been able to gather and analyze data fast and accurately. A talent that had guided her decision to focus on market research within the company.

"Which is probably why Sigmund has been calling every day since he sent them over. I don't know how many times I had to tell him that you were on vacation."

Korey was a recent college graduate with an eye for detail and excellent fashion sense. Today he wore black slacks, suede shoes and a black button-front dress shirt with the sleeves rolled up to his elbows. Normally that look proved too casual and just slightly messy for Riley, but Korey made it appear classic.

"Get him on the phone. He has to do better. We're paying him too much money and we've got way too much riding on this for him to flake on us now."

"No problem. Let's see, it's about seven in the morning his time, but he should be up."

Riley flipped back to the first page and paused when her stomach made an unruly sound.

"Or should I wait until after you've ordered some dinner?"

Korey also thought he was a comedian.

Riley turned to him ready to frown, but her stomach made the sound again and she felt the beginnings of a headache. Crap!

She turned her wrist and looked at her watch. It was almost seven. She'd been in the office since six this morning and her last meal had been at noon.

You need to make time to take care of yourself. Eat. Rest. Live outside this office.

The words rolled through her mind as if her mother were standing right in front of her. Marva Gold was a stern but loving mother. She'd had to be to raise four children—three boys and one girl—in the shadows of the glitz and glamorous world of fashion. She was also the commanding force behind the Gold Foundation, which provided scholarships and other programs for marginalized youth through-out the US.

"Schedule a call for first thing tomorrow morning. I want to speak with him before my meeting with RJ. We have huge orders for this collection and if he hears Sigmund isn't sure how many of those orders he can fill on time, he's gonna flip."

Riley circled back to her desk and sat in her custom-made ergonomic chair. Two years ago during an annual physical, her doctor mentioned how much she worked, and when she hadn't been able to promise to cut down, he'd suggested she make work as comfortable as possible. A chair that didn't have her back and neck aching every day was an improvement. Not a big enough one, but at least she was trying.

"Does that mean we're getting out of here before nine tonight?"

"Is that a complaint I hear?" Riley didn't bother to look up. She'd dropped the report on her desk and immediately started looking at the sketches that had been scanned into the presentation for tomorrow's meeting. These were the designs that would be fea-tured in her segment of their first show of Fashion Week. RJ and the rest of the production team would be studying them for the umpteenth time tomorrow. Then they'd look at the models wearing the gowns and make the final decision for which ones would be in the show. Nervous didn't quite explain how she was feeling right now.

"Not a one," Korey continued. He held his tablet in one hand and typed as he sat in the chair across from her desk. Probably sending Sigmund an email about tomorrow's phone conference.

"But I was thinking I could probably make it to at least drinks for the dinner party I'd planned to attend."

She did look up at him then.

"Why didn't you say something? You didn't have to stay here with me tonight. I could have managed without you." Despite her reputation, Riley was not coldhearted and she didn't treat people like they were trash or beneath her.

She was friendly and easy to work with. At least, that was what Korey said after being here almost six months. The two of them had hit it off during the interview, on a day that had begun horribly for Riley. The fact that Korey had been able to make her laugh and focus on something else besides whatever headline had been floating around at that time sealed his fate as her new assistant.

He was essentially the closest thing she had to a friend.

"Nope, my job is to be here when you're here and it pays me well." Korey finished the email and looked up at her with a pointed smile.

Riley grinned but then sighed as her temples throbbed. "I need an aspirin."

"Maybe you need to have dinner and go to bed. We've been in the office past nine every night since you came back from Milan."

"It's crunch time." That was the excuse she'd been giving herself these past seven days each time thoughts of that night in Milan crossed her mind.

"True."

She'd expected him to say more, but instead he continued to stare at her.

"What?"

He shrugged. "I'm just debating where the line is at this moment."

Because she knew what he was referring to, Riley gave him a reassuring look. "You're safe."

Korey looked relieved as he leaned forward, resting an elbow on his knee. "What happened in Milan? You left focused and intent but came back a little… off."

"What?" Panic sliced through her with a sharp edge. "I'm the exact same."

Korey's hands were up immediately, waving back and forth. "No. No. Not in a bad way. Absolutely not, you're always on point. Always. There's just a little difference. Like how quickly you were able to admit you've been here too long tonight. If this were last month you would have been determined to push through."

Milan hadn't changed her.

One night did not make a difference to her life.

"I can admit when I'm tired." It was the safe reply. "That's all it is, Korey. So you can go get your drinks. And I don't care how drunk you get, I want you here tomorrow at six. Not a second later."

"Now, that's the prevacation Riley talking." Korey chuckled and jumped up from his chair because prevacation or not, he knew it was only safe to cross the line temporarily.

"See you in the morning. Have a fun evening."

Fifteen minutes later she was still sitting in the same spot.

Had she changed because of the night she'd spent with Chaz? Because that was the only thing that had been different about this year's vacation. After thinking on it another few seconds Riley slammed her palm on the desk and shook her head. It was just sex, damn!

She shut down her computer and grabbed her bag and purse before leaving the office. She wasn't different. Korey was overreacting, something he did frequently. He was lucky she liked him like a little brother and that he was so organized and knew a great pair of thigh-high boots when he saw them or she would have definitely fired him a thousand times by now.

Minutes later Riley stood at the elevator feeling smug because that last thought sounded much more like her. If she *were* acting any different, that was. But she wasn't. Everything was the same as it had been before she'd gone to Milan. All she had to do was keep telling herself that and it would be true.

By the time she made it to the garage Riley was shaking her head. She was pitiful and she hated to admit it. She wasn't the same since Milan because now she couldn't get Chaz and the feel of his hands on her body out of her mind. And as if her thoughts weren't traitorous enough, her phone dinged with a text message notification. When she read the text, saw who it was from, her heartbeat quickened and butterflies danced a happy little jig in her stomach.

Chaz hadn't been his usual self today.

Or the day before, or even the day before that. In fact, he could admit that he'd been thinking about Milan—or rather a very enjoyable twenty-four hours in Milan—much more than he'd assumed he would.

It wasn't like he didn't have anything else to do. Chaz just couldn't get Riley out of his mind. But when he looked up to see his uncle walking into his office unannounced, he hoped there was some business issue the man needed to discuss that would help Chaz focus on other things.

His uncle began as soon as he sat down. "I heard Ron sent his little girl to Milan to snatch Perry off the market."

Well, this wasn't going to go the way Chaz thought it might.

Tobias King was a big man, six feet three-and-a-half inches—two inches taller than Chaz—two hundred and eighty-something pounds. Chaz was only partially guessing. He'd gone to Tobias's last doctor's appointment to make sure his uncle's blood pressure was in check. High blood pressure was a silent killer and with the stress of the company and seven ex-wives, Tobias was always borderline and terribly neglectful when it came to his health.

Now that Chaz was in New York for a while, he would make sure his uncle took better care of himself, even if it meant treating Tobias like he was a child.

"It's not a big deal," Chaz replied. "You've got a good design team and they're coming up with fresh and innovative ideas. This men's collection is going to speak directly to professional millennials and they're gonna love it."

Chaz was certain of that fact because he'd spent hundreds of hours researching this demographic and studying the look, price and packaging of their clothes. He'd kept a few employees that were in the branding department when he came, but he'd hired half a dozen more to create a team that would produce quickly and efficiently.

"But she's a slick one, that Riley. Polished and primped all the time and smart as a whip. I've heard her talk at conventions and the rare times she speaks to the press. She's got her father's attitude but her mother's look. A dangerous combination."

Tobias was going bald but wasn't quite ready to shave his head, so he kept the remaining hair cut very low. He'd even taken to wearing fitted hats and had designed a collection of them with matching casual jackets. His low-cut beard was white, giving him a distinguished older-gentleman appeal, while his steely deep brown eyes remained as astute as they'd been when he was in his twenties.

"She's not that bad." The moment he said those words, Chaz regretted them.

Not actually *regret*—that was a word Chaz didn't allow himself to associate with. He believed everything happened for a reason and that when things didn't go the way he planned, he just had to reconcile himself with that reason. Still, those weren't the words he'd meant to say and now he'd have to deal with the backlash, which he had no doubt was coming swiftly.

"How do you know how bad she is? Did you run into her while you were in Milan? I hoped you wouldn't when I found out she was down there."

"I've known Riley for a few years now, Unc." Chaz had always called him "Unc" instead of Uncle Tobias. It was shorter, and to the nine-year-old who had been grieving his parents when he first came to New York, the less he had to say, the better.

"Yeah, well, this was the first time she's been direct competition to you."

Chaz shrugged. "I didn't go to Milan just to meet up with Perry. And we actually did get a chance to talk. He was meeting with RGF this week but that doesn't mean he's officially working for them."

"Oh, he is. Look at this." Tobias slammed the fashion magazine onto Chaz's desk.

It was open to an article naming Perry this year's hottest and most desired designer. And first on the list of fashion houses Perry wanted to work for was RGF.

"We're fine. PR's getting the buzz out about the lines we're pushing this season and the sales projections are seventy-six percent higher than this time last year."

Tobias grabbed the brim of his red hat and pulled it off. "It's gotta work. We've gotta get back on top."

"We will. Don't worry," Chaz told him.

Tobias shook his head and walked toward the door. When he turned back, he extended his arm and was waving his hat at Chaz as he talked. "Keep an eye on her. She's planning something big."

Chaz didn't hesitate. "You didn't bring me here to watch what anybody else is doing. King Designs is in a class by itself and I'm going to make sure nobody forgets that."

Tobias drew his lips into a tight line and gave a curt nod before leaving Chaz alone. Twenty minutes later when he'd deemed work impossible, Chaz drove his Mercedes GLS back to his apartment. Once he'd showered and changed he sent the text that had been on his mind all damn day.

Have dinner with me.

CHAPTER EIGHT

CHAZ WAS WAITING for Riley. He sat at the table near the window and stared out at the unfettered view of Manhattan. There was a chill in the air and they were calling for snow, but from sixty-two stories up, the city looked perfect.

The white tablecloth, two long white candles, sparkling crystal and silverware and the small glass vase with two red roses were perfectly arranged on the table. He'd rented the entire upper level of the LeGrange restaurant to preserve their privacy. The lights had been dimmed and in the far corner near the bar a man played jazz on the piano.

Chaz was hungry, but he wasn't worried. If Riley hadn't accepted his dinner invitation, she would have returned his text message telling him so. Standing him up would have been too normal and Riley was anything but that. In fact, Chaz was almost certain she would have taken pleasure from personally declining his offer. The thought made him smile. Riley was competitive and proud and she did not like a dare. Even a subtle one such as having dinner with him. The whole suggestion was taking her out of her comfort zone, something Riley would not like but would be unable to resist for fear of being thought of as less than.

The latter part was what Chaz hated. The moments when he knew Riley was doubting herself despite the confidence that wrapped around her like a winter blanket.

A new text message from Chaz's driver told him that Riley was on her way up. Chaz motioned for the server to pour the wine.

Because the room was empty Chaz could see straight across to where the elevator doors opened. When she stepped off, he stood.

Another server had been waiting at the elevator and he accepted Riley's long black coat and ivory scarf. She kept her cream-colored purse with its gold chain strap and gold RG emblem on the front. Riley wore a long chocolate-brown pencil skirt with a matching jacket that was belted at the waist and fastened with a large button at her left shoulder. Her pumps were four-inch heels, increasing her five-foot-seven-inch height until she would be almost nose to nose with him.

She stopped in front of him, piercing him with her steady gaze. Chaz smiled and offered her a glass of wine. "Good evening."

Riley accepted the glass but did not smile in return. "Good evening."

"You look stunning as usual."

She sipped from the glass. "Thank you. What are you trying to do?"

Candid. No-nonsense. Sexy.

"I'm trying to eat. Haven't had anything since lunch so I'm starving. Here, take a seat so we can order our food." He pulled out her chair and waited the few seconds while she contemplated if she were, in fact, going to have this meal with him, or if she'd just shown up to tell him his "date" was not acceptable and how far she planned to go, before she finally sat.

Chaz went to his side of the table and sat across from her. He took the black napkin from the plate and spread it over his lap.

"You know that's not what I meant."

He handed her a menu. "I'm aware. But I figure we can talk while we eat. I'll answer all your questions and then you can tell me how your day went. Or I can start and tell you I'm thoroughly tired of meetings."

The server arrived, and Riley gave him her order without looking at the menu. Impressed, Chaz followed her lead but ordered a bigger steak and a baked potato instead of asparagus. He was just finishing a sip of his wine when the server left them alone and Riley's question came firing back.

"We said twenty-four hours. That was it. You were not supposed to contact me again."

She sat with her back straight, shoulders squared, and her tone hadn't gone a notch above casual. He almost smiled because there were so many things about this woman who captivated him.

"I was still at work and I had a feeling you were, too. We both need to eat." He let his hands fall to his lap instead of shrugging.

"Before Milan we ate separately. I expected we would continue to do so."

Chaz had expected he'd get back to work at King and take care of a few things regarding the launch of his new app. He hadn't thought he'd want to see her as badly as he did.

"Relax. We're having a meal. There's nobody here to see us and run back to tell the world. It's just you, me and the steak I can't wait to taste." It really was that simple. Chaz frowned as he thought about how many times he'd wanted to pick up the phone and call her or even send an email or text in the last week but hadn't done so because he'd known she would have this exact reaction.

They were consenting adults keeping in touch with each other—that should not have been a problem.

"You know what the tabloids would say. Not to mention our family."

"Stop."

The single word came out much stronger than he anticipated, but the quick close of her lips and the second of shock that flashed in her eyes was exactly the response he wanted.

"I've said this before and I'd really like not to repeat it again. That feud is between my uncle and your father. It's ridiculous that you and I, or your brothers and I, or any of us for that matter, would carry it on like a torch to be passed through the generations."

She opened her mouth to speak but Chaz held up a hand, stopping her. "I wanted to see you, Riley. I wanted to talk to you again. To spend some quiet time with you after a really long week. That's all."

Instead of replying she removed her napkin from the plate, opened it and placed it on her lap. Neither of them spoke for a few moments. Chaz figured she needed the time to gather her thoughts. She had two choices: get up and leave, or sit here and deal with the dinner and conversation. He was positive she would opt for the latter since he knew she'd had his driver take her home to change clothes before coming. No way would she have gone through all that if she didn't want to see him, too.

As the music played in the background Chaz thought he saw her moving her head to a familiar song.

"You know Nancy Wilson?" It wasn't like the musician was playing popular music. Chaz had requested jazz because it soothed him.

"My mother has all her albums in plastic on a shelf in her sitting room. Just a few years ago she finally agreed to stop playing them and let Major have the songs digitally remastered and added to a playlist for her. Now if she's not working, she has her headphones in while she sings along to Sister Nancy. That's what she's called her since I can remember, as if they were long-lost friends."

A soft smile covered her face and the leeriness Chaz had about her not relaxing enough to enjoy this dinner dissipated. It was obvious she loved her mother dearly. Just speaking about her had brought an air of contentment around her that Chaz didn't see often enough.

"Both my parents liked jazz. I remember it playing in our house all the time. When I came to live with my uncle, I didn't hear it as much. He was more of an R & B kind of guy. But when I got my first MP3 player, I downloaded every jazz song I could find." He still remembered how excited he'd been to see the songs on his playlist. For days that was all he'd done—lie in his bed and listen to the music because it made him feel closer to his parents even though he knew they were never coming back.

"Your parents died when you were young, right?"

"Nine." He'd been young and scared to death of what would happen after the social worker and the police officer arrived at his house to tell him and his babysitter that his parents' car was hit head-on by a drunk driver.

"I'm sure that was tough. But your uncle took you in and you seem to have turned out well."

He chuckled. "Gee, thanks."

She waved a hand. "You know what I mean."

"Yeah, my uncle and his wife, Arlene—she was number four—they came to pick me up from the neighbor who had let me stay there temporarily so I wouldn't have to go into foster care." Saying those words after twenty-four years seemed odd.

"Wait, his wife's name is…Veronica. Right? She loves fur." She reached for her glass and Chaz watched her slim fingers grip the stem.

"Veronica is number eight, and yes, she loves fur. It's all over the house." He had to shake his head because the memory of Veronica's redecoration of King Towers, as it would always be known to Chaz, was almost horrific.

"For the record, I'm not totally against fur," she said after a quick drink.

"I'm not, either. But she definitely missed the 'less is more' lesson."

Ahh, there was that smile.

"You are not wrong about that," she replied with a chuckle.

The server brought their food and conversation died for a few minutes. The steak was phenomenal, and when he looked up in between bites, he realized the company was exactly what he needed.

"I've been inundated with meetings," he said between bites. "Juggling the design work with the new app I'm launching is more tiring than I thought it would be."

She dabbed the napkin to her lips. "An app? I thought you owned a social network site."

"That's where I started but Conversation Media's sort of morphed into a few other directions. ChatMe is our new subscription-based platform and it's launching in three weeks."

"Is this one for singles, too? How many dating sites does the world need?"

Chaz could have taken offense but he was growing accustomed to Riley's biting candor. There seemed to be absolutely no animosity in her words, just simple statements that meant what they meant.

"This project is geared toward millennials, and no, it's not specifically for dating. But let's not talk about that." He knew the moment the words were out she detested them.

"Let's not." She picked up her knife and fork, cut a piece of steak and slowly put it into her mouth.

He watched her lips moving and instantly thought of when they'd been wrapped around his dick. He dropped his hands to his lap and kept his gaze focused on her.

"What?" she asked when she finished chewing.

He shrugged. "Never thought the sight of a woman eating could be so sexy until now."

She looked like she was going to discontinue the meal but then shrugged just as he had, before cutting another piece of steak and putting it into her mouth. She liked him watching her. Her fingers shook slightly as she held the fork and guided it to her mouth. At the same time, color darker than the blush she wore fused her cheeks. He hadn't planned on this but he couldn't help it—his dick had grown so hard in the last few seconds, pressing firmly against his zipper, Chaz had no choice but to move his hand to cup the bulge.

She finished that bite and licked her lips. He resisted the urge to groan. He desperately wanted to release his painfully hard erection and beckon her to wrap her mouth around him one more time.

"Your food is going to get cold." She lifted her glass to her lips and treated him to another peek of her tongue just before the deep red wine slid smoothly into her mouth.

"I'm no longer hungry for food." It was an honest reply, one that was hitting him with more force than he'd considered. Each time he'd thought of her this past week he'd recalled their time together in Milan, the sex and the talking. Tonight he'd craved both but had no idea the physical could be so jolting or encompassing.

"But wasn't that what this was about?" She cut a

strip of asparagus into three pieces and speared one piece with her fork.

Chaz's gaze had gone to her plate, anticipation beating with his heart as he waited to watch the food go into the warm cavern he wanted so desperately to slip his dick inside.

"This is about so much more," he admitted.

This was insane.

And empowering.

Riley walked into her penthouse with Chaz a few steps behind. She dropped her keys and purse on the table a couple feet inside the foyer and reached for the buttons of her coat. His hands were there immediately, coming around her to pull the coat from her shoulders.

"The closet is over there," she said with a nod to the left.

She moved deeper into the apartment, hearing him opening the closet door and envisioning him hanging her coat and then his own. Her heels clicked on the glossed wood floors and she went to her pale gray sectional to take a seat at the far end. She picked up the remote from the glass end table beside the couch and touched the button that would activate the window blinds. A low hum echoed off the twenty-foot ceilings as black custom-fit blinds came down over the floor-to-ceiling windows.

"You buy the penthouse with the best view of the

city but use blinds to close it out," he said as he sat on the other end of the couch. He was across the room from her now and the sight of him relaxing in her apartment gave her pause because she'd never had guests, other than family, here before.

During the ride from the restaurant to her place Riley had resigned herself to the fact that they would have sex one more time. It might be smarter, but it was definitely futile to ignore the attraction between them. Besides, from the moment she saw him standing beside the table in the dining room of a restaurant he'd rented solely for their privacy, she'd known she wanted to be in bed with him again.

"I've seen this view all my life." It was an even reply that she did not believe required more conversation.

"And the blinds keep the outside from coming in."

He didn't bother to phrase that as a question. He probably knew she wouldn't answer if he did.

"It's a great space. I can see touches of you all around."

So they were going to have chitchat first. She could do that. Although she'd wanted to straddle him when he'd cupped his erection in the restaurant, and when they'd rode in silence, she'd wondered what it would feel like if he slid across the seat and slipped his hand up her skirt.

"I hired a decorator."

He nodded. "Who knew you well."

He stood then and walked around. Her style was contemporary, the colors in this area of her home were soft gray, crisp black and cool white. There was glass, sterling silver, light-colored wood flooring covered in the center by a plush gray rug.

Chaz was in her space. His tall, broad form seeming to dominate the area. He wore a black suit, slim-fit pants and a jacket, stark white shirt that added casual to the professional, shined Tom Ford loafers and a stainless steel Tag Heuer watch on his left arm. She was more than intrigued by the deep hue of his skin, the strong edge of his jaw and the shadow of a mustache and beard he wore.

"This is an interesting piece."

Riley was not pleased by the instant pang of awareness she felt when he turned to face her, holding the phallus-shaped rose quartz in his hand. The soft warm color of the crystal against Chaz's dark clothing was a jolting contrast that put Riley on edge.

"I liked the color." That wasn't what she wanted to say. It wasn't how she wanted to say it. She sounded like an idiot.

Chaz looked down at it, holding it in his hands in the same way he'd held his erection.

"A paperweight?"

There was amusement in his tone.

Riley jumped from the couch and crossed to stand near him by the mantel where the piece—the Heart, as she'd called it—had been placed.

"A decoration," she said and reached for it.

He moved his hand just out of her reach.

"A decoration that sparks something in your eyes."

She looked away from him but that made her feel like a coward, so she returned her gaze to meet his. "I use it when I meditate. The healing properties of the crystal assist in seeking calm and restoring energy." She left out self-confidence and contentment because he didn't need to know that she fought hard to maintain those things. And he definitely did not need to know that the idea of meditation had come from the therapist she'd been seeing for the past three years.

"Does it work?"

His fingers were still wrapped around the crystal, palm toward the wider base, thumb rubbing over the smooth tip. Her pussy throbbed and her heart rate increased.

"How frequently do you meditate with it?"

She swallowed when she finally looked up from his fingers to meet Chaz's gaze. His eyes had grown darker, his voice deeper.

"That's private," she said in a tone that also seemed huskier.

"There's no one here but me and you. Show me, Riley."

No. She couldn't. It was a ritual she'd developed for herself. A safe space that refilled her when she struggled, empowered her when she felt weak and

comforted her when the privacy she craved began
to strangle her.

He stepped closer and took Riley's hand. He kept
his eyes locked on hers while wrapping her fingers
around the crystal. It was warm from his touch and
the intense sexual energy he exuded seeped into her
palm. He was silently daring her to share this very
intimate part of herself with him. She shouldn't, but
she wanted to.

Snatching it from his hand, Riley walked away.
When she realized he was still standing in the same
spot, she looked over her shoulder and asked, "Are
you coming?"

CHAPTER NINE

SECONDS AFTER ENTERING her bedroom, Riley lowered the blinds. She placed the crystal on her bed and turned on the lamp on the nightstand. After moving to the stand on the other side of the bed she turned on the second lamp, and the room was cast in a warm glow.

Chaz stood in the doorway. Riley pointed toward the beige couch adorned with pillows near the window.

"The best view is from over there," she told him.

He moved in silence over the beige carpet.

Once he was seated, Riley stepped out of her shoes. She placed them neatly at the end of her bed instead of going into her closet as she normally did. There was nothing normal about this night. She unzipped her skirt and pushed it down her legs, noting the soft scrape of material over her nylon-covered legs. The jacket came next and she folded the garments, draping them over the end of the bed. When she chanced a look at Chaz, his gaze was riveted on her. A warm tendril of desire slipped slowly down her spine. Her bra, nylons, the thin wisp of lace panties were all removed and Riley climbed onto her bed.

Her meditation routine usually included candles and the tracks of crashing waves and trickling springs she had programmed to a special playlist. Tonight there was only Chaz.

Her heart thumped so loud she thought for sure he could hear it from where he sat about twelve feet from the bed. She lay back against the pillows, closing her eyes briefly and then opening them to stare up at the ceiling.

She could do this.

More important, she wanted to do this.

Extending her arm, Riley grabbed the crystal. She closed her eyes and focused on everything from the feel of it against her palms, to its shape and its purpose. Surprisingly, the desired calm came over her even though she was not alone. She could hear the waves in her mind and feel the warmth of the sun against her bare skin. And the crystal began to warm. It started to feel familiar in her hand, but not only because she'd used it so much in the past year. It felt like another phallus she'd held just a week ago.

She needed to clear her mind of everything but her happy place. Search for the good within herself and within the world that surrounded her.

That was what she did whenever she meditated. It was her purpose in taking solitary time to aid in her healing. But tonight she couldn't find that place. There was a new goal in her mind and right now it felt closer than peace and healing. She didn't have to search for it because it was there in the room with her. In her hand and across the room.

"When I close my eyes you're there." It was a quiet admission spoken just before she took the crystal in one hand and rubbed the tip over one tight nipple.

"I'm here right now."

She hadn't expected him to speak, but with the sound of his voice, her pussy throbbed and she spread her legs wide.

"You're a distraction." Riley circled the crystal over one nipple while the fingers on her free hand toyed with her other nipple. On one she squeezed tight, pulling and tugging until her breathing came faster. The other was being massaged by the warm crystal. Her breasts felt full, sensation moving from each nipple down to her gut, settling like a pool of hot lava at her center.

A soft moan escaped before Riley could pull back. She wanted to do this but at the same time she didn't want to share too much, to show him anything deeper than a physical reaction. Her mind and her body fought to control which would be revealed.

"I can't go."

Why did she enjoy his voice so much? Her legs moved over the soft material of her champagne-colored comforter. She wanted him inside her, buried deep and thrusting powerfully until she couldn't breathe, think or care. Riley took a deep breath and exhaled in a slow but shaky whoosh of air. She moved the crystal to the slope between her breasts, trailing it down her torso and stopping at her navel.

"You can't stay." The words came out in a whimper. They needed to be said out loud because her body wanted nothing more than for him to join her on this bed, to take her to that sweet place where she'd soared a week ago. She missed that place. Every day this week she'd thought about it and missed it more. Too much. She'd berated herself for the thoughts but tonight it was a simple truth.

"Not after tonight," she whispered. "Not again."

She moved the crystal lower until it slid along the shaved skin of her mound. Riley loved the sensation of being shaved—each touch felt a million times stronger, and she experienced each lick on a deeper level. It was amazing. It was also one of the things that gave her a sense of power over her own pleasure. With one hand she parted her folds and with the other she dragged the crystal over the slickness of her clit, down past her opening and back again, letting the coolness of the crystal mingle with the heat from her arousal.

With the crystal in one hand, she slipped two fingers into her aching center, gasping at the stretch and moaning with the pleasure streaking wildly throughout her body. She lifted her legs, flattening her feet on the mattress, and pumped her fingers in and out while circling the crystal over her clit. Her head thrashed on the pillows, teeth clenched tight. He wasn't speaking but he was there. She could smell him and feel him in the heat that swirled throughout the room.

This wasn't how her meditation usually happened. It wasn't the feeling she normally sought. But this was good, too. In fact, it was magnificent. Her heart raced with the thrust of her hands. Her hips moved with the motion and Riley knew her release was near. She could feel it in every jolt of her thighs, the full sensation in her breasts. She heard it in the sound of her fingers moving against her coated walls, her essence dripping down between the crevice of her bottom and onto the bed.

"I'm right there with you."

His voice was an intrusion. A pleasurable one.

"You look so damn beautiful, Riley. So strong and talented. The way you know exactly how to find your pleasure. You didn't let me stop you. You're in your own world bringing every sensation that you need."

His words rolled around in her mind but they were hard to comprehend through the fog of desire. She was panting now, arching her back as she drove her fingers deeper.

"Damn! You're so wet. So pretty and wet. I can't stand it."

Riley couldn't, either. She needed this to end. She

needed to fall over that cliff and float once again, to let the pleasure take her away. She dropped the crystal, using fingers from one hand to work her clit faster while the other hand continued to pump fiercely inside until her legs shook and a deep guttural moan eased from her throat.

"Riley! What are you doing to me?"

His voice was clearer now, in the few seconds just before her body stilled. Her release was intense, touching every part of her body, keeping her eyes closed tight, her fingers locking where they were, her toes curling into the comforter.

"Chaz!"

She hadn't meant to say the name that seemed to be etched into her mind. She'd never called out a man's name during sex, or during meditation.

Coming down from her release was like falling onto a bed of cotton. Riley sighed into the softness, relaxing her mind, body and soul.

Loud moaning caught her attention and she turned her head to see Chaz through pleasure-blurred eyes. He had removed his jacket. His legs were spread wide, the button, belt and zipper of his pants were undone. His dick was in his hand, thick and long and dripping with his release as he made one final jerk and cursed long and loud.

Moments later he was gone and Riley closed her eyes, ready to welcome a deep sleep. It wouldn't be the first time that a meditation session had lulled her into slumber and she hoped it wouldn't be the last. But just when she started to slip into dreamland, she felt him touch her.

"What are you doing?" she asked when Chaz's strong hands and arms moved under her and lifted her from the bed.

"Helping you get cleaned up."

"No." She pressed a hand into his chest just in case he didn't believe she was serious. "I can do it myself. I don't want your help."

A muscle in his jaw twitched and Chaz continued walking. He stopped at the bathroom door.

"I wasn't going to go in with you, Riley. I know you much better than you think."

He set her down, and when her feet touched the floor, Riley backed away from him.

"I hope you don't mind but I used one of the washcloths in your closet."

Because he'd needed to clean up, as well. Her gaze dropped briefly to his now-zipped pants. His shirt was unbuttoned but his chest was covered by a tight black tank. She looked back at him. "Thank you."

"You're welcome," he replied, and Riley stepped into the bathroom and closed the door.

Chaz had admitted to Riley that he couldn't leave. What she didn't know was that he'd meant more than just physically getting up to leave her bedroom. By that time he'd had his dick in his hand and his desire to see how far they would go to find their pleasure was a top priority. But aside from that, something else held him to her. It was the oddest and most intense feeling he'd ever experienced. He wanted Riley physically but there was also this nagging desire to just be with her.

Chaz didn't want to "be" with any woman. Committed relationships, live-in girlfriends, long-term associations, none of those were his thing. And not just because he'd made a name for himself as one of the world's top bachelors—that was a persona he'd facilitated to grow his business. Now that Conversation Media was a global success, he didn't have to sacrifice so much of himself to sell the brand. The problem was that he'd adopted a lot of the professional persona into his personal life over the years. It worked for him because he'd watched relationships come together and inevitably fall apart. His uncle was on wife number eight and he was only fifty-seven years old. That wasn't a promising scenario for Chaz.

Riley stirred and he leaned down to kiss the top of her head.

It was morning. He'd spent the night in Riley Gold's bed, in her penthouse, with her wrapped in his arms. They hadn't had sex. The meditation/masturbation session had been enough to wear them both down. Chaz sensed their very busy workweeks had contributed to that, but he wasn't about to debate the issue.

Last night he'd watched her come out of the bathroom with a perplexed look on her face. He hated that she'd fully expected him to leave. As if he could share something so intimate and thoroughly enjoyable with her and then walk out without saying a word. It dawned on him later that he'd done that many times before with other women.

He was wearing only his boxers when she returned, and when he extended his hand for her to join him on the bed, Riley had simply walked around to the other side and climbed in. She turned out the light on her side and Chaz lay down and turned down the light on his side. Seconds later he'd pulled her into his arms and there she'd stayed all night.

"I don't know how to do the morning after," she whispered.

Chaz rubbed his hand up and down her arm, enjoying the feel of her soft skin. He'd been doing that all night. Touching her, smelling her, taking in every aspect of this woman who he'd thought he knew.

"Neither do I," he replied. "How about we make it up as we go?"

"How about we just get up?" she said and started to move.

Chaz did not want to let her go. He did not want this mood to be over. It was beyond what he'd imagined having dinner with her would be. That both unnerved and excited him.

She shocked him by dropping a quick kiss on his chest before pushing up and away from him. Her curse came next.

"I'm late. Dammit! I have a meeting with RJ and a conference call with my distributor and I'm late!"

Riley jumped out of the bed. She snatched a peach-colored silk robe from the chair and thrust her arms into it as she moved across the room.

Chaz sat up in bed. "You're an executive, Riley. You can definitely cancel a meeting."

She was already across the room, pushing a button on the wall to open the door of a massive walk-in closet. "I'm not canceling. This is important. We've got deadlines and he's trying to say he can't produce the numbers we've already presold. It's a catastrophe and I have to fix it."

She was talking while moving up and down the aisles in the closet. From what Chaz could see there were more than a dozen aisles of clothes. He could only see the first row of shoes but figured she'd have just as many shoes as she did clothes. Straight to the back was a wall of accessories. Riley came out with clothes and shoes, a necklace dangling from her fingers and a look of sheer panic on her face.

Chaz eased out of the bed. "No worries. I'll call for my car. He'll get you there in no time."

"But what about you?"

Chaz walked toward her, not giving a damn about the morning hard-on tenting his boxers until he stopped in front of her and watched her gaze dip down.

"I'll get a cab or I can wait here until my car comes back. You should get your shower. He'll be here quickly after I place the call."

She looked back up at him. "Ah. Yes. Shower. I should do that. Thank you."

Chaz grinned and leaned in to drop a quick but soft kiss on her lips. "Stop thanking me, Riley. If I'm sleeping with you I can certainly make sure you get to work."

She pressed her hands against his chest. The chilly links of her necklace eased over his bare skin.

"So we're sleeping together?" Her eyes were wide with concern but Chaz didn't detect any regret in her tone.

"Yeah. After last night I'd say we are. You cool with that?"

She swallowed and blinked and then squared her shoulders.

"I believe I am. As long as we're discreet. This cannot get out, Chaz. It has to stay between us for however long it lasts."

Her tone was adamant, which told him that was the line and he needed to decide if he dared to cross it. Not today.

"I can do a private affair with you, Riley." He

wrapped his arms around her waist and pulled her to him again. "I can do just about anything with you."

Every part of her relaxed and a smile touched her lips.

"I can do a private affair with you, too, Chaz."

She came up on the tips of her toes and kissed him, tilting her head as her tongue met his. He was instantly dragged into a heated and sensual moment that was going to change both of them forever. She pulled away first and looked at him for a few muted seconds before going into the bathroom. Chaz stood there, trying to wrap his mind around what had just happened. Then he grinned.

He was having an affair with Riley Gold.

CHAPTER TEN

"ARE YOU OKAY?" RJ asked as Riley stood from the conference room table and began pulling her sketches together. The drawings had been spread out along the table after the PowerPoint presentation. Then the models had come in wearing the designs and she, RJ and several other members from the production team had gotten up to inspect each one personally.

"I'm fine," she said. "The beading on the Elisa gown needs work. Everything about this line rests on the details. It was in the sketch so I'm not sure why it didn't translate into production. I may just write a memo to the production team. That way they'll all know to pay closer attention. But the gown will be ready by the first show so there's no need to worry about that."

RJ was perched on the side of the table as he listened to her, and when she came close enough, he grabbed her arm to stop her from moving.

"I wasn't talking about the gowns, Riley. I'm asking about you."

Her brother was six years older than her, tall and slimly built. He had a deep voice just like their father, but he was also overprotective and prone to hovering just like their mother.

"You came in late this morning. Very late."

"So you want to dock me? I'm here at the crack of dawn every day, even on Saturdays, and I stay well into the evening every night. I don't take sick days and only one vacation per year. Come in late one morning and I'm being scolded like I'm a slacker."

She yanked her arm away from his grasp.

RJ put his arms up in mock surrender. "Whoa. I'm just asking as a concerned brother because I know how hard it is for you to go off script. Which is why I wondered what happened when I called your office and Korey told me you weren't in yet and that he hadn't heard from you."

Riley was now snatching the sketches off the table. When she grabbed the final one, she smoothed the stack and slipped them into a case.

"And now you're brooding because you don't like to be wrong." RJ chuckled. "Come on, Riley. Just tell me that everything is okay and I'll leave you alone. I can respect your privacy."

Her head snapped around at those words. "Liar. You probably already called Mom and Dad to see if they'd heard from me. And then you would have found Major and Maurice in whichever woman's bed they awoke in this morning to question them."

He chuckled. "As a matter of fact, I called Major and Maurice first."

Riley shook her head. The Gold twins were infamous for their identical dashing good looks and their prowess with almost every woman they encountered. They were also a part of the Babysit Riley Club, in which each of her brothers proudly held membership.

"That was so unnecessary. I was just a little late." She'd been an hour and a half late because she'd been sleeping too soundly and too comfortably in Chaz's arms.

"But you're never late."

That was true.

"I apologize."

"No need to apologize, Ri. You're entitled to some time for yourself. It's just that we know you, and when something changes, we worry. But I'm glad to see you're just fine and on top of things with this new bridal collection. Your reports are amazingly detailed and the plan you've mapped out for marketing is stellar. I believe we have a winner here."

That sent happy vibes throughout her body. "I'm glad to hear that because I want to revisit the specialty shops idea again. I know Dad said he didn't want to detract from our flagship stores in Manhattan, Beverly Hills and Paris, but I really think these smaller, more focused shops will hit a section of the market we're missing."

They'd had this discussion before at meetings with her father; his top two designers; Major, who was the technical developer; Maurice, who was in charge of public relations; and Janel Lindsey, the CFO. The same conversation had also been held during family dinners at their parents' house. Each time, her idea for expansion on a smaller scale was shot down, regardless of her market research on the idea. The Gold brand was big; everything they did had to be big or they didn't do it. That was what her father insisted.

"You know how Dad feels about that."

"He's wrong." She knew she was being adamant, but she couldn't help it. She was positive the idea could succeed. Riley hoped that with the successful launch of this couture bridal collection, she could convince her father that she really did know what she was doing.

"Well, let's just take on one thing at a time. The projected sales numbers for the Golden Bride Collection look great and the campaign you've outlined is amazingly thorough. If the marketing department follows through with everything you've pitched here, we're looking at a major victory for the company." RJ seemed pretty excited by that thought.

Of course he was—more sales meant more accolades for him. Not that he needed them. As the firstborn he was going to slide into the CEO position at RGF the moment their father retired. Major and Maurice didn't want that job. But Riley could see herself doing it. She'd also seen herself as a phenomenal chief executive of market research and she knew that she was ruling that position right now. So RJ could have the CEO spot, Riley planned to make her mark right here and right now.

"I have to call Sigmund again. I missed our call this morning. But I need to stress the importance of having enough stock to fill all the preorders. Once the show is over, stores are going to need dresses to sell."

"Maurice will have all the online specs ready to go so ordering will be possible," RJ added.

"I don't want there to be a wait for delivery in the first few weeks of the launch. I want brides to see these dresses, fall in love with one and plunk down their cash to buy it. And I want them to have their dresses in hand well before their wedding dates so they have more time to adore it. Especially since they'll only have it on for one day."

RJ eased off the table and went to grab his notepad and empty coffee cup. "There's my sister. For a while I was wondering why you were going so hard on this collection when I knew weddings were not your thing."

Riley picked up her half-full bottle of water. She tucked her tablet under one arm and held the sketch case in her hand.

"Oh, you know I'm never getting married. But I can relate to a woman's dream of the perfect wedding."

Probably because she'd had it once, a long time ago. Even before Walt, Riley had dreamed of what her wedding would be like. The problem with that dream was that she'd never really thought there would be a man who she wanted to marry. Blame that on the low self-esteem that had plagued her throughout her teenage years, which she'd finally overcome when she was in college. She'd taken a chance with Walt because it was a good business match and she had liked him in the beginning. The problem was marriages shouldn't be built on "like"—or infidelity for that matter.

"Well, you've conveyed your thoughts to the design team and they've come through in spades." RJ led the way to the door.

"They did. I'm really pleased with everything they've done."

"The show's going to be great. Rehearsals are already planned to start early next week."

"I'll be there," she said as they walked down the hall, past conference rooms and mini fitting spaces, where designs could be examined and altered.

"You know, Ri, you don't have to do everything. I feel like you've been trying to make up for what happened with Walt and that's just not necessary."

It was. Calling off the engagement had cost the company a lucrative deal with one of the world's top clothing distributors. On top of that, her parents had been friends with Walt's parents for a very long time. The breakup had been about more than just her and Walt. It had severed a business connection and a friendship. Right or wrong, Riley carried that guilt.

"I should have never agreed to marry him. The entire relationship was a mistake. One I plan to never make again."

"Well, you know how I feel about relationships, so you'll get no argument from me. But I would like to see you socializing a little more. Going to parties just to have fun instead of reeling in designers for the company. Taking more than one vacation. Sleeping in one morning because you work too many long days and nights in the first place. You know, stuff like that."

He nudged her when he finished and grinned.

Riley smiled back while shaking her head.

"I know you're not talking. You are the biggest workaholic of us all." Which was true. Major and Maurice were the most relaxed of the Gold siblings, while Riley and RJ took the job, the company and their family obligations much more seriously.

He shrugged as they moved to the elevators. "You might be right about that, but I do at least take the time to go on a date here and there. You're on this solo crusade when I think a little socializing might be good for you every now and then."

"Wait a minute. Are you, my big brother, telling me to find a guy to sleep with?"

"Whoa. Oh no! Full stop! That is not what I said. Let's just change the subject."

Riley chuckled at RJ's completely over-the-top but hilarious reaction as they stepped into the elevator.

"Yeah, I think changing the subject might be a good idea," she said and laughed a little more.

"What's your vision for ChatMe? Do you see yourself finding the woman of your dreams through your singles app?"

Chaz was momentarily taken off guard by the question. He hadn't custom designed a singles app. That had not been his vision at all. And the part about finding the woman of his dreams... Just no.

"ChatMe will be a hub for a certain demographic to socialize, share their triumphs, issues, goals, etc. The app was never intended to be just about dating." He gave the response in a smooth and relaxed tone even though on the inside he was irritated by the question.

Maybe because Riley had said something very similar last night.

"Okay, I hear you." The interviewer's name was Valeria and she was the owner of a popular blog and YouTube show. She was pretty and had already expressed her personal interest in him prior to requesting a formal interview.

Chaz had declined the personal invite but accepted the professional one because her blog and show had over two million subscribers.

"But you have to admit that your following in the past few years since you blew up on social media has been women. Many of whom are looking for a way to reach out to you personally."

Valeria had a sly smile, sea green eyes and a mass of curly hair. A week ago, Chaz would have slept with her. Today he was simply trying to get through this interview.

"Social media is all about making connections. Business networking, friendships and, yes, even committed relationships have been born from the many platforms out there. At Conversation Media our goal has always been to start conversations. ChatMe will do the same on a more focused level. We're excited about its formal release in two weeks and hope you'll join us for the launch."

With that, Chaz stood. He buttoned his suit jacket and said, "We're done."

Valeria stopped her recorder and hurriedly stood, as well. "Ah, okay. I hope you weren't bothered by the questions. Inquiring minds want to know." She attempted a joking tone but Chaz really wasn't feeling it.

"It's fine. Can you just let my PR people know when the interview will be posted?"

"I really wish you'd let me do a live show, Chaz. I'm sure we would've gotten thousands of viewers if we'd gone that route. Maybe you'll reconsider for the week of the launch. It'll be double exposure for you on the blog and the broadcast."

Chaz started to walk away. "As I stated before, that's not possible. I'll be tied up with pre–Fashion Week events during that time."

"Oh, right, the favor you're doing for your uncle. That's so noble of you."

"There's nothing noble about what I'm doing. King Designs is a family business that put me through private schools and college. My loyalty will always be to my family." Chaz wasn't sure why this woman was irritating him so much today. He just knew that the sooner he could get away from her, the better.

"Well then, I'll be sure to let your people know when I post the interview."

He didn't miss the bite in her tone and he understood the real meaning of her words—she would post when she felt like it.

"I appreciate that. We have a vigorous lineup of promotion on all media platforms beginning early next week and going into the month after launch, so we'd like to keep track of all of the places we need to thank for their support."

And if she wasn't one of them, he would have to accept that, but Chaz had never allowed a reporter to take advantage of him or to play him for their own personal reasons, and he wasn't about to start now.

His phone rang and Chaz said goodbye to Valeria before walking out of the room.

"I was able to move the first run-through to one thirty but we've got models, makeup artists, hair stylists and photographers on the clock," Chaz's assistant said when he answered.

"I'm on my way. Getting in the car now."

Chaz ended the call and stepped into the elevator. Minutes later, he was walking out of the building and onto the sidewalk filled with New Yorkers on the move.

Guy, his driver, had already stepped out of the black town car and was opening the back door for him to get in. Chaz slipped onto the backseat and pulled up his text messages. Nothing from Riley.

He wasn't sure if that was a good or bad sign.

CHAPTER ELEVEN

ONE WEEK LATER, Riley walked into the 11 Howard Hotel, ready for *Saturday Style* magazine's style summit, which officially kicked off the pre–Fashion Week festivities. She wore a navy-blue wool coat that complemented her navy-and-rust geometric-print blouse, pleated skirt and calf-high cognac-colored suede boots. Her hair was pulled back into a neat bun.

One of the hostesses took her coat and Riley tucked her purse under her arm as she walked toward the ballroom alone. Since this event used the best technology on the market to showcase the hottest trends in style, Major was also attending. He had a front row seat as did Riley, but she hadn't wanted to be up front during the presentation so she'd arrived late, hoping she could avoid immediate detection and slide into a seat at the back after everyone had been seated.

Two minutes after she walked into the auditorium her plan failed miserably.

"Hello, beautiful."

"Hi." She tried to make sure her response wasn't as breathless as she felt upon seeing Chaz again but wasn't convinced it had worked.

The room was dark but with the bright blue, fuchsia and white lights coming from the stage and the large screens displaying the presentation, she could tell that he looked good. His suit jacket was dark, his jeans light, button-front white print shirt crisp.

"It's been another busy week," he said. "I didn't get a chance to catch up with you."

"Yes. I know. There's a lot going on right now. I'm just going to go and find my seat." She moved around him and was not totally surprised when he extended an arm to stop her.

"Hold on a sec. Can we just talk for a minute?"

"The show's already started."

"You knew that would be the case when you purposely arrived late." He sounded like he was making a casual observation.

His arm was extended in front of her but he wasn't touching her. She could still feel the heat emanating from him. It was familiar, and to her chagrin her body sought it.

"Five minutes, Riley. We can go out into the hall or find some other private space."

How much would she love to go off to some private space with Chaz? Way too much, to be honest.

She shook her head. "Not here, Chaz. Maybe we can meet up later."

Before he could respond Riley saw two people coming up the aisle heading directly for the spot where they stood. She moved around his arm and walked quickly to find any available seat. It was best if she sat down and got out of view.

After the show it took Riley a few minutes to make her way out of the auditorium. Reporters and photographers were everywhere and while she knew it would be good to be seen by one of them and to offer a tease about RGF's show, Riley couldn't help but hope they ignored her. Besides, Major was here—he could just as easily give a tease and a lengthy interview since he wasn't opposed to using the tabloids at every opportunity. He figured that served them right for all the times they purposely misinformed the public with outright lies.

"Hey! Riley Gold is here! We were wondering if you were somewhere in this crowd!"

Once again her plan was foiled as she locked gazes with a reporter. Riley didn't remember his name but she knew that he wrote for the *Fashion Insider* blog. He was tall and slim and wore too much product in his hair.

"Hello." Riley clasped her purse with both hands and held it in front of her as if it were a shield.

"What can you tell us about RGF's upcoming show? I know you've got something up your sleeve. The gossip mill's been buzzing, girl, so please give us an exclusive!" He looped his arm through hers and walked them past a throng of reporters who had snagged their prey and were chatting away.

The lobby of the hotel suddenly felt very crowded and Riley tried to focus on saying the words she'd typed into the notes app on her phone on the drive here.

"You'll just have to wait until the show for the full surprise," she began. "Of course, we'll be having our annual media brunch on the seventh, where you'll be treated to delicious food and face time with our top designers."

"Oh yes, I already have my invitation. But what we really want to know is if RGF will be focusing exclusively on a debonair men's collection. Or are you unveiling something extra special for the women this year?"

He was persistent. They all were, and when Riley glanced around the room to see more people stopping and talking, her heart began to race.

"RGF always offers top-of-the-line designs for everyone. We've built a platform based on quality and high fashion for a diverse world and we plan to deliver just as we have in the past."

"Okay, so you're not going to spill any of the details. You're always so discreet." He smiled at her and Riley took that moment to step out of his hold. She put a little space between them and was prepared to say her farewells and get the hell out of there when he continued.

"Unfortunately, that didn't work well where Walter Stone was concerned. We were all saddened by that breakup, but I'm sure not as sad as your parents were. That was a pretty lucrative deal hinging on those nuptials. But all that's water under the bridge now. Do you have anything you'd like to say to Walt and his new fiancée? I hear they're planning a fall wedding. Will RGF be designing the bride's gown? Or is that a little too close to home since you and Walt were once an item?"

Riley's legs began to wobble and her knees threatened to give out. She squeezed her purse as if she thought she could actually tear the leather apart with her rage. And still, she smiled.

"I wish Walter and his bride-to-be the very best. I'm sure she'll be quite beautiful in whatever she wears. Now, I'll have to say good-night."

She started to leave and he tried to grab her arm. Riley turned quickly, giving him a glare that had him immediately withdrawing his hand and attempting a faint smile. He stuffed his hand into his pocket and backed away. Riley left him standing there and headed to the bathroom. She wasn't sure she would make it out front for the valet to bring her car.

Pushing through the door, Riley went straight to the last stall. She eased the lock in place before leaning her back against it. Her eyes closed and tears threatened to fall. That reporter was an ass and he did not deserve her tears, but, oh, how that rock sat in the center of her chest, threatening to bury her alive.

She focused on her breathing and the fact that the

anxiety attack could not last forever. In very slowly, out even slower. In and out. It would end and she could continue on with her life because she was a survivor. Her fingers eventually stopped clenching her bag and held it loosely instead. Her stomach still churned but she could swallow now without feeling as if she had a throat full of cotton.

Her phone buzzed from inside the purse and Riley jumped at the sound. She took another breath and opened her eyes, feeling confident that no tears would fall. After digging inside her purse she found her phone, relieved that it was just a text and not someone on the other end. She didn't know if she was ready to talk just yet.

Drinks at my place?

Riley read the message and let her head fall back against the door. She closed her eyes again and wondered what was going on. Reporters were asking about Walt and his fiancée, when she hadn't even known Walt had a fiancée. She was sleeping with the enemy and enjoying it far too much. And Production still wasn't giving her a definite on her preorders. When exactly had her life become so chaotic?

And would drinks with Chaz make it better or worse?

She looked down at her phone and began to type.

My place, 20 minutes.

* * *

When Chaz rang the doorbell, Riley opened the door and pulled him inside. She closed the door and turned to wrap her arms around his neck before taking his mouth in a kiss that scorched every part of him.

His arms went around her waist, hands flattening over her ass and back. She tilted her head, taking the kiss deeper, and he went with her lead, stroking his tongue against hers and pressing her against his now-growing arousal. She lifted a leg, dragging it up the outside of his, moaning into him as if he were giving her everything she wanted and needed right now.

It felt good. It felt damn perfect. His body reacted instantly, dick pressing against his jeans in a hurry to get deep inside her. Her breasts were plastered against his chest. She moaned and sighed as she momentarily pulled her lips away from his. Her teeth nipped his lower lip before she sucked it into her mouth. Chaz held her tighter. He gripped her ass until she gasped, and he was just about to push her skirt down and take her against the wall right in the foyer of her house. But he stopped.

Chaz pulled back from the kiss. He kept his arms around her but looked down at her face instead of moving away.

"What happened?"

Her makeup was gone, her face freshly washed

and simply gorgeous. And her hair was down. Messy and hanging past her shoulders. He continued to survey her and noticed she'd removed her boots and taken off all her jewelry. Her eyes were dry, not red at all, but there was a weary look in them. A dead giveaway that something was going on.

"Nothing." She tilted her head. "Did we really need the preamble of drinks? Aren't we old enough to know how this is going to play out?"

"No and yes," he replied. "I'm also smart enough to know when a woman is using sex to mask her pain or discontent. Now, tell me what happened."

She pushed away from him and walked into the living room, going straight to the bar in the corner near the window.

"You can go if your plan for tonight was to talk or cuddle. I'm not in the mood."

Chaz could have figured that out without her saying so. He walked slowly into the living room, watching her quick, irritated movements as she took a glass from the cabinet and placed it on the bar top with a loud clunk. She yanked off the top of a decanter and poured more than half a glass of whiskey. He stopped a few steps from the bar and slipped his hands into the front pockets of his jeans. Riley looked directly at him, brought the glass to her lips and tilted her head back to swallow. Three big gulps and she almost emptied the glass. With a shaky sigh she lowered it and held her lips in a tight line.

"Don't you stand there and judge me," she warned.

Chaz shook his head. "Never. But I would like you to tell me what happened to put you in this mood."

"Why? So you can fix it? I'm not in the market for a savior, Chaz."

"I'm not in the business of saving people, Riley. But when I'm sleeping with a woman, I like to know she's taken care of physically and mentally. So I'm asking you again to please tell me what happened."

He couldn't phrase it any nicer, not while trying desperately to hold on to the temper brewing at the thought that someone had upset her.

She set the glass on the bar top and folded her arms across her chest.

"It's stupid." She shook her head and blinked rapidly.

Chaz knew that if a tear fell it would be the end of him.

"If it hurt you, it's not stupid."

"I'm over it," she snapped. "Over him and all his lies. Have been for a long time now. It was just that slimy reporter. He knew exactly what he was doing asking about the show and then slipping in the comments about Walt and his bride-to-be. Like

I give a damn what that woman's going to wear to her wedding."

Chaz felt partial relief in knowing that it had only been a reporter who aggravated her, and deep irritation that her mood involved her ex-fiancé.

"He's a reporter—their job is to push buttons. They get a reaction or a blurted quote and they run with it. You know how this works, Riley."

"Yeah, I do and I think it sucks."

"I agree." Chaz moved to meet her on the other side of the bar. He really needed a drink now.

She pushed the whiskey closer to him and he found a glass and poured. He took a gulp, letting the liquid burn the back of his throat before he spoke again.

"What else did he say about you and Stone?" Because that was all that mattered to Chaz. He could not care less if the jerk was marrying someone else.

"It's not relevant. I shouldn't have let it get under my skin. Like you said, I know better."

"But you continue to expect people to be better. That says a lot about you."

It also said she was probably going to continue being bothered by people who didn't have the good sense to get a clue.

"It either says I'm an idiot or I should have just punched the guy and went about my business."

"You're not an idiot." Chaz finished his drink and

turned around to lean his back against the bar. "Were you in love with Stone?"

It shouldn't matter, but it did. He was certain Riley had the capacity to love. What he didn't know is whether or not she'd given her heart to someone before.

She looked down at her glass and then up to him. "No. I wanted to be. Not just because it would have been the perfect professional union, but because it would mean that I was normal."

He shrugged. "Normal is overrated."

"Says the guy who played varsity football since he was in the ninth grade and went on to be a big shot in your fraternity."

She'd done some research on him. Chaz was flattered.

"It's much harder to be different."

She sighed. "We were supposed to be like the royal couple of fashion. Everybody was watching us and waiting for the big day. And all the time I was having daily anxiety attacks and cringing each night he decided to sleep with me."

Chaz had a rule about not knowing the past details of his current lover's sex life. But something made him want to know everything possible about Riley.

She lifted her hands and ran her fingers through her hair. What had been smooth and neat earlier was still mostly straight at the top but curling on the ends.

Chaz recalled how soft those curls were when he'd run his fingers through them. He wanted to do so again.

"I wasn't frigid in bed," she said in a huff.

"I can attest to that." He leaned over and nudged her shoulder with his.

She looked up at him with a semismile.

"Anyway, on the business end everything went very well. Stonemill Apparel was going to cut our distributing costs in half because of their global reach. At the time we had contracts with a US and UK distributor locked down. However, we'd entered into intense negotiations with Canada and China. Stonemill had warehouses and networks all over the globe. It made sense to combine all our distributing to one company. The process would be streamlined, contracts, payments, shipments would all be the same across the board instead of our production department having to navigate the different logistics of each separate company."

Chaz agreed. "A very smart idea."

"And because we were also combining our families, the company names, our brands, it was going to be a huge slam dunk in the industry."

"I remember." His uncle had been beside himself with worry over how the Gold/Stone joining was going to affect his distributing.

"And I didn't want to mess that up. I wanted RGF to not only remain on top, but to be so far ahead of the other fashion houses that they could only dream of catching up." She sighed and shook her head. "But I messed up."

Chaz rubbed a hand over her back and ignored the quick jolt of tenseness he felt in her with the touch. "You didn't mess up. You made a choice. A very good one, I would say."

She drank the rest of the whiskey, setting the glass down with another loud clunk when she was finished. "He cheated on me. I mean, I suspected all along that he had someone else but I'm not the type to hunt for clues to bust some guy. I was, however, the type to think once the wedding was over, it would stop. But there's something about having proof slap you in the face. That was a defining moment for me."

"And for Stone. It defined him as a jackass."

She nodded and turned so that she was now leaning her back against the bar just like him. "And it made me the Ice Princess. But I'm fine with that as long as RGF stays on top. As long as I continue to do a good job for our company. Next week will be another defining moment for me. The launch of our new lines, the marketing plans, the promotion, the sales, all that success will hopefully erase the whole Ice Princess title and all the negative energy that goes with it. But then this goofy reporter throws it right back into the mix and I begin to shatter like a piece of glass."

Chaz stepped in front of her. He cupped her face in his hands and tilted her head up slightly to stare into her eyes.

"There's nothing fragile about you, Riley. You are the strongest, most goal-oriented and beautiful—on the inside and out—woman I know. No matter what that reporter or any other reporter says, I know who and what you are. But more important is that you know who you are and your family—the people who love and care about you—know. Everyone else, all those people who believe what's printed on those blogs and in the papers, are idiots and don't warrant a second of your time."

Her full smile came slowly. The light it ignited in her eyes shone brightly. And the warmth that speared straight through Chaz's heart spread wildly.

"You're great for my ego."

"Oh, really? Well, I'm glad I could be of some use."

She eased her arms around his waist and pulled him closer. "I know of another way you can be useful."

Chaz grinned. He let his hands slide away from her face, moving them down to her waist, where he planted them and lifted her up to sit on the bar. "You're not the only smart one in this room, Ms. Riley Gold. I can think of more useful things I can do, as well."

"Oh, really?" She reached behind her back and

undid the snap at the back of her blouse before lifting it up and over her head. After tossing it to the floor she cupped a hand behind his head and pulled his face close to hers to whisper, "Show me."

CHAPTER TWELVE

THIS WAS WHAT she needed tonight. Riley let her head loll back as Chaz's mouth and tongue created a scorching hot path down the line of her neck, over her collarbone and between the valley of her breasts. She moaned and whispered his name when he unhooked her bra and cupped her heavy mounds. Her legs were spread wide and wrapped around his waist, her hands plastered to the back of his head to stop him if he dared try to discontinue the sweet torture.

"Just do it," she crooned before sucking her bottom lip between her teeth and biting down in an attempt to hold in some of the desire bristling through her at the moment. The battle was lost the second he closed his mouth over one nipple and palmed the other breast.

"Yes. Take it. Take it all." Riley arched into him, loving the hard suction of his mouth and the quick scrape of teeth over her sensitive skin.

He held the other breast in his palm, squeezing and releasing. Damn, she was on top of the bar in her house, a place she'd never dreamed of having sex.

Chaz pulled back and she groaned until his strong hands found the band of her skirt. In one quick motion he lifted her slightly off the bar, just enough to pull the skirt and her panties down and off her legs. The marble top was cool to her bare ass as Riley watched Chaz remove his jacket. She reached forward and grabbed for his shirt, yanking it so hard the buttons popped free. She pushed it over his massive shoulders and down his arms. He reached back into his wallet to find a condom while her hands moved busily over his belt buckle, button and zipper. She pushed the jeans and his boxers down as far as she could reach and heard him ripping the condom packet open.

"Now," she whispered when her thighs began to tremble.

Her pussy ached for attention and her chest heaved with anticipation.

He sheathed himself and wrapped one arm around her waist to pull her closer to the edge of the bar top. She locked her legs around him again just as he thrust deep into her. They both yelled out at the quick and forceful meeting. And then he was pounding into her, taking her higher, faster than she'd ever imagined.

"You are everything," he groaned. "So hot and tight around me, so damn wet, Riley."

Riley was wet and he was easing in and out of her with a friction that touched every sensitive spot she possessed. At this moment her body was his and he was owning it completely. This was what she needed—to lose herself so completely.

"Harder!" Her hands clamped down on his shoulders, blunt-tipped nails digging into his skin. "Harder, Chaz! Take me harder!"

He obeyed her command, pumping into her so hard and fast their joining made a cupping sound that echoed throughout the room. She was going to fall right over the edge. She could feel her pleasure rising so high it had no choice but to fall gracefully. Or rather ungracefully as she yelled out his name the second her body trembled with the force of her orgasm.

"Yes!" Chaz yelled with her. "Give it to me! All for me, Riley. Give it all to me. Yes!"

She couldn't have withheld it if she tried. Her legs shook around him, her arms trembled and her teeth almost bit hard into her lip as pleasure ripped through her like a tornado. He'd slowed his thrust only marginally, his arms going around her back, holding her tight against his chest as her essence poured over him.

His quick pace resumed moments later when her body was still filled with the hum of her release. He buried his face in the crook of her neck and pumped wildly into her as if he couldn't hold back a moment longer.

"Riley." Her name tore from his lips.

His teeth brushed over her skin.

"Riley. Dammit, Riley!"

His arms grew tighter around her and Riley locked her ankles at his back. She pressed closer to him, enjoying the sound of her name in his husky tone.

"You can come for me now," she whispered, wanting him to do just that.

To empty himself into her so that they could be even and one. That was a jolting thought and before she could marinate on it any longer a painfully raw sound ripped from Chaz's throat.

"For you!" he groaned and pounded into her so fast she grew breathless. "All. For. You."

Riley's head jerked as he punctuated those last words with deep and powerful thrusts that almost pushed her right over the bar. If he hadn't been holding on to her so tightly she was sure she would have toppled over, but he *was* holding her. His arms were wrapped tightly around her as he pushed his dick into her and held completely still for endless seconds. The pounding of his dick as his release pulsed into the condom had her legs trembling.

Her back was arched and Chaz lowered his forehead to her chest. "Just you, Riley."

The words were spoken slowly as he pulled slightly out and pushed back inside her. "Just you."

She showered alone and Chaz used her guest bathroom.

After a few minutes, he stood at the sink and

splashed water over his face once and then again in an attempt to clear his mind. When that didn't work, Chaz grabbed one of the soft yellow towels from a rack and pressed it to his face. It smelled just like Riley—fresh, clean and impossibly feminine. He sighed as he pulled it away and looked into the mirror.

"What the hell are you doing?"

His deep brown eyes looked the same. The strong jaw and light dusting of a beard, the scar just above his eyebrow he'd had since he was six and the precisely lined shape-up he'd received earlier today at the barber—all of it looked the same. The man he'd always seen was staring back at him. And yet Chaz knew that was a total lie.

As he stood in Riley Gold's guest bathroom all he could think about was going into her bedroom, getting into her bed and cuddling with her until they both fell asleep. He wanted to sleep with her again. Not sex. Sleep. Him. And Riley Gold.

That wasn't something he would have even considered before.

It was insane.

And it was the truth.

He cursed.

This wasn't the type of affair he'd envisioned when he proposed this idea. He hadn't anticipated that feelings would go along with the mindless sex. And he knew that hadn't been Riley's plan, either.

Yet, here they were sharing things about themselves they'd never intended to share with anyone. It was wild.

Talking to Riley the way he had, comforting her, feeling the overwhelming need to find Walt Stone and beat him senseless, none of that was part of an affair. At least, not in his world. Chaz was about his job, his company and living a drama-free life. It was what he'd worked so hard to achieve since he became an adult and it wasn't negotiable. He had to get back on track.

At least, that was what his mind was saying. Other parts of him—the foreign part that never usually had a say where women were concerned—was leaning in a different direction. And for the first time in his life, Chaz didn't know what to do.

CHAPTER THIRTEEN

TWO DAYS LATER, Riley was still thinking about Chaz. To be honest, she hadn't stopped thinking about him since returning from Milan. No matter how much she'd tried to deny it, the man was on her mind every day. And even more on the mornings after they'd been together. Luckily for Riley the last two days had been filled with meetings, reports and other Fashion Week festivities that had kept her and Chaz pretty busy. So busy that they'd resorted to communicating mostly via text messaging. That was why Riley's phone was now on her desk only inches away from her keyboard as she reviewed the yearlong sales projections for the Golden Bride Collection.

Riley noted the time on the bottom of her computer screen and pulled her glasses off to rub her eyes. She'd been reading and taking notes for the last three hours. It was almost four in the afternoon and she toyed with the idea of getting out of the office at a decent hour today. But there was still so much work to get done before that was an option.

She eased her glasses back into place just as a brisk knock sounded at her door.

"Come in!" she yelled and reached for the half-empty bottle of water on her desk.

"These are for you."

Riley stopped drinking abruptly, spilling a few drops of water onto the bold orange, white and blue striped sweater she wore. Her high-waist pants were beige with an orange-and-blue plaid print. Thankfully she was sitting close enough to the desk that water didn't trickle down to her lap.

"For me? From who?"

Her heart thumped and Riley fought the tendrils of panic steadily trying to creep into her mind.

Korey sat the large bouquet on her desk and snatched the card that had been attached to a long white pitchfork thing in its side.

"Let me see," he was saying and making a big production out of pulling that card from the white envelope.

Riley had no idea what came over her but she hopped up from her chair and hurried around the desk in time to snap the card from Korey's hand. She held it without looking at it.

"I'll read the card later," she said. "The hand-crafted veils were supposed to arrive today. Can you track them down so we'll be ready for the meeting with the designers in an hour?"

Korey frowned and Riley knew why. He wanted

to know what was wrong with her. While her assistant hadn't dared to ask her that question again, Riley knew he was still wondering. She could tell by the way he looked at her daily when he thought she didn't notice.

"They're beautiful." Korey watched her closely.

"They're flowers," she replied but sighed when she looked at them because they were gorgeous.

She wasn't a romantic by any stretch of the imagination, but this large bouquet filled with exotic-looking flowers and crisp greenery was exactly what she would like to receive if she were inclined to receive such gifts. Only she had no idea who would have sent them or why. She was certain it wasn't Chaz because they were simply having an affair. There was no romance involved, even though that candlelight dinner with just the two of them had been really close to a real date.

"I need to speak with you, Riley."

The booming voice had both Riley and Korey looking toward her open office door. Ronald Gold, Sr., blocked the access with his broad frame and piercing gaze.

"I was just leaving," Korey said, offering Riley an apologetic look before hurrying out of her office.

Riley slipped the card into her pocket. "Hi, Dad."

Ron closed the door behind Korey and walked the short distance to where Riley was standing in front of the desk. She'd moved in an attempt to block the flowers. Her father came close and first tweaked her nose before pulling her into a tight hug.

Riley melted into the hug, wrapping her arms around her father's expansive build. If he hadn't gone into fashion, her father could have definitely been a professional wrestler. In addition to his build, Ron's imposing stature and voice gave him an air of command. But when it was just the two of them, when his large arms were around her and holding Riley tight, he was just her dad.

"Somebody's sending my baby girl flowers?"

Riley hurriedly pulled out of his embrace and turned to look at the flowers again.

"I don't know who they're from. Korey just brought them in seconds before you arrived. But, anyway, what's going on? I thought you and Maurice were out making the rounds at all the preshow events this week." There was nothing, not even sports, her father loved to discuss more than the fashion empire his father had built.

"Probably one of the manufacturers or the boutique owners that want to carry our new collections."

She hadn't thought of that and felt a wave of relief now that her father had put that possibility out there.

"You may be right. So what brings you here? I sent the latest projections via email this morning. I'm going over long-term numbers now."

Ron reached inside his black suit jacket and pulled out a rolled-up newspaper. He slapped it down onto the desk a few inches away from the floral arrangement.

"I called his editor this morning and very strongly suggested an apology be printed first thing tomorrow. We are not here to be used for their amusement."

Riley refused to let her fingers shake as she picked up the paper and read the first few lines of the article.

Riley Gold wishes her ex and his soon-to-be wife well, but won't be designing the bride's dress.

She tried to swallow but it was hard. Instead she focused once again on breathing and surprisingly her breaths came easier, sooner, than she'd anticipated. She shook her head.

"I thought the guy only ran a blog, not that he had a byline at this trashy tabloid, as well. Anyway, I suppose he had to find something to take up space."

She dropped the paper into the trash can on her way to the other side of her desk. Ron was already pacing in the space that she'd left vacant and Riley sat in her chair.

"Not at our expense! I made it clear they would never get another interview or invitation to any of our private events if they didn't have an apology on the front page tomorrow morning. The editor is old-school but needs the readers so he was hesitant, said his guy got a direct quote from you."

"He did." She leaned forward and rested her arms

on the desk. "He stopped me after the style summit and asked about the collection. When I wouldn't tell him, he brought up Walt and his fiancée. He asked if we were designing her dress. I told him no and that I wished Walt well. Which is the absolute truth."

Riley had decided a few years ago that wishing him dead wasn't going to change what had happened.

"Don't give them ammunition, Riley. How many times have I told you that?"

"If truth is ammunition, then I might as well yell 'no comment' every time I see a reporter coming toward me. Look, Dad, I know what they're doing. They're trying to bait me, ruffle my feathers, throw me off my game. I'm not going to let that happen."

Ron stared at her seriously for a moment before chuckling and shaking his head. "Stubborn. Just like your mama."

Riley sat back in her chair, for the first time in her life truly feeling unbothered by Walter Stone and his childish antics.

"I've just got better things to do with my time. We're about to break records with this upcoming show."

Her father took a seat in one of the guest chairs across from her desk. "That's exactly what I want to hear. Tell me more about what you've done, baby girl."

Riley was happy to talk about work with her father. She wasn't thrilled that at twenty-nine years old he was still calling her his baby girl, but there was nothing she could do about that. Ron Gold wasn't the type to change until he was good and ready.

The idea to construct a runway in the center of an old railway station was brilliant. It was the perfect backdrop for the rebranded King Collection, which was King Designs's signature men's collection. Tobias King and his team of designers had always been known for their cutting-edge, streetwise men's clothes. But in the last two years that line had fallen behind women's couture and wedding wear. Chaz was aiming to change that.

"It's important to have the lighting coordinated with the music and the specific beats of the show. I don't want any lags and every model must be specifically highlighted when they get to the front of the runway." Chaz had been giving instructions all day while they worked at the venue. It was nearing six in the evening and he was just hitting his stride.

Ram, one of the three show producers, was nodding as he took notes on his tablet.

"Four rows of seats, not five. Three sections of seating and the remaining guests will be standing. We have a lot of room for people to move around, and if they're standing too far in the back or near the bar during the show, that's why we have the screens. The idea is to make this feel like a night at the club, not a high-end fashion show."

"Got it. Alexa's working with the backstage manager. They were having some deep discussion about where to place the rails and the chairs for the models. The designers are with hair and makeup, going through a hair and makeup test."

"As soon as that's complete I want everyone out to do another run-through. Have the designers stand down here and to the sides so we can get an idea of how everything is going to look. What's the status of the rest of the set? We only have six more days for construction." Chaz walked the length of one half of the U-shaped runway.

"We normally deal with the show producers."

Chaz turned at the sound of another man's voice. He held back a frown when he saw Lenzo Fuchetti, one of King's top designers.

"I know what's normally been done, but normal wasn't working for this particular line. So this time around we're switching things up." Chaz normally worked well with the staff, whether at his company or Tobias's, but Lenzo had a particularly hard time dealing with Chaz's presence and the amount of impact he had on this upcoming show. Chaz could relate to an extent. Aside from his relationship to Tobias he was an outsider. His specialty was in a totally different industry. Still, Tobias had paid for Chaz's education, which had given Chaz the tools to create his own multimillion-dollar brand. The least Chaz could do was use some of what he'd learned to help his uncle get back on top. If Lenzo didn't understand, that was his problem.

"We'll need sheer drapes at the back, pin lights as well as spotlights," Lenzo continued.

Chaz nodded to Ram, approving what Lenzo said. Ram made note of it and Lenzo huffed. There was some commotion at the front doors and Lenzo hurried off to assist.

"I have an engagement at seven. We need to get on with the run-through," Chaz told them.

"I'll get everyone together," Ram told him before walking away.

Chaz ran a hand down the back of his head and sighed. This had been a really long day. It had also been the second day of not seeing Riley. He didn't like that. And when he reached into his back pocket and pulled out his phone, he didn't like that she hadn't sent him a text since earlier this morning. He scrolled through his emails quickly, wondering when he'd become so concerned with whether or not a woman had texted him back. Normally women waited for him to return their messages. He frowned down at his phone for a few minutes more, wondering if he should break routine and text her again.

He didn't have time because they were ready to do the run-through and getting this finished in the next hour was important.

Forty minutes later they were entering the last minutes of the show. The run-through was going

smoothly with two other designers on-site making
a few suggestions and changes to the models' hair-
styles and positioning on the runway. Chaz happily
stood to the back to let them do their thing. His job
was the overall picture. Making sure everything
he'd been working on with the designers and his
team for the last six months had been implemented.
All of that made the arrival of four models on the
stage wearing wedding gowns even more discon-
certing.

He moved closer to the runway, where Lenzo was
now directing. The shorter man was clapping his
hands and motioning for the models to come to the
spots he pointed to immediately. His midnight-black
hair was shaved on the sides and left to hang long in
a curly strip down the center, and he was constantly
pushing the strands out of his eyes.

"This one should be front and center. So you
switch places with her. Yes, just like that. And then
turn slightly." Lenzo looked back to the booth where
the lighting guys were sitting. "I want the beading
to sparkle. Shine the light right on her so that she
glitters throughout the room."

"What the hell is this?" Chaz asked. He'd spent a
few seconds trying to come up with a less irritated
way to ask why these models wearing dresses he'd
never seen were on the runway, but he couldn't.

Lenzo turned to face Chaz, annoyance evident in
the narrowing of his eyes and the smirk of his lips.

"It is high fashion. I don't know what these others have done to appease you and your specialty branding idea, but this is what we do here at King Designs."

Chaz didn't really have a problem with the dresses. They were fine from a cursory glance. What he didn't like was someone attempting to usurp his authority.

"The first portion of this show is dedicated to the unveiling of the men's line—fifteen new designs. There are seventeen women's designs that will follow. We specifically decided to focus on ready-to-wear designs for this showing, waiting until next year to present haute couture pieces. Therefore, King Designs isn't offering any bridal wear this year."

Lenzo sighed heavily. "It's the spring/summer season—that's precisely when we would unveil such one-of-a-kind bridal designs."

Again, Lenzo's logic was not totally wrong, but Chaz's rebranding plan called for King Designs to do the unexpected. Lenzo turned away from Chaz and continued to instruct the models. Chaz took another moment to gather his thoughts. Then he went into action.

"This run-through is over." He spoke loud enough so that everyone in the room stopped what they were doing and looked at him. "Thank you, models, stylists, supervisors. We'll see you again on Monday." He turned to look at Ram and said, "Shut the place down for the night and make sure it's locked up tight."

Lenzo, because the man really was an idiot, continued, "I'm not finished."

Chaz leveled his gaze at him and spoke with as much control as he could muster. "Yes. You're definitely finished for tonight."

Lenzo's shocked expression didn't faze Chaz as he turned and walked out. In the car on his way back to his apartment Chaz called Tobias to explain what happened and suggest a course of action to deal with Lenzo's blatant disrespect for not only him, as an executive of the company, but also for the plan approved by Tobias, the CEO. His uncle agreed. On a heavy sigh Chaz admitted he was tired and needed to unwind. He was grateful for tonight's engagement, and with that thought checked his text messages again. The one he'd been waiting for had finally come.

Be there at 8.

CHAPTER FOURTEEN

RILEY SAT IN the backseat of the car and read the card one more time.

208 Lenholake Avenue, 7:00 p.m.

She had no idea where this was or what she would find when she arrived. All she knew was that after her father left her office this afternoon she'd sat at her desk staring at the flowers and wondering if they could be from a vendor or a cruel joke from Walt. Finally, she decided it was ridiculous to keep trying to figure it out when the flowers had come with a card. She'd pulled the card out of her pocket and read it, the cryptic nature surprising and irritating her. But just when Riley was going to chuck the card and the flowers into the trash she looked at the arrangement one more time.

That was when she saw it.

The vase was made of rose quartz. Faint white lines mixed with the pale pink of the urn-shaped container.

The vibrant colors of the tropical flowers—deep orange, purple and fuchsia—along with the dramatic greenery had completely captured her attention from the moment Korey brought them into her office. Riley hadn't paid any attention to the container, and as she'd reached across her desk to touch her fingertips to its cool, smooth surface, she'd smiled.

And immediately left her office to go home.

Chaz hadn't texted her all afternoon, so when she'd come out of the shower, she sent him a simple message: Be there at 8.

The car pulled up in front of what looked like a regular building around the corner from New York's acclaimed Fifth Avenue. Riley stepped out when the driver opened the back door. She grabbed the lapels of her peach coat closer as a chilly breeze blew and she stepped onto the crimson-carpeted section of the sidewalk. A green awning covered the walkway and displayed the building's address in stark white numbers.

Riley was still unsure of what she was walking into. The address attached to a lovely flower arrangement in no way expressed what tonight was about. She'd dressed according to her mood and with comfort in mind—black-and-white leopard-print wrap skirt with a peach-colored blouse and knee-length black suede boots. Her hair was pulled back in a stylishly messy knot and she carried a peach-colored leather bag she'd picked up when she first arrived in Milan.

"Good evening. May I take your coat?"

The older man had approached quietly. Dressed in an excellently cut black tuxedo complete with stark white shirt and bow tie, he looked every bit the stately butler. That was when Riley really surveyed her surroundings. The foyer was bright, with cream-colored walls, intricate molding and an immaculate marble floor. To her left was a double-height windowed gallery and a sweeping staircase.

"Madam?"

"Oh. I apologize," Riley said when the butler had stepped closer, his hand extended for her coat. She removed the coat and handed it to him.

"I believe I'm supposed to meet someone here. His name is—"

The butler had taken her coat and folded it neatly over his right arm. With his left he held up a finger, which had Riley snapping her lips shut.

"Right through there, madam. You will find everything that you are in search of."

He walked away as quietly as he'd come, but Riley watched him until he disappeared through a side door the same color as the walls. What was this place?

She walked in the direction she was told, choosing one of the two doorways that were separated by a remarkable antique grandfather clock. The room she entered was even more astonishing. The walls were a bold celadon with butter-colored floral-print wallpaper beneath the chair rail. That was just the beginning of what she thought might be eighteenth-century Parisian decor, which was definitely not her taste. The best thing about the room were the magnificent views of Central Park through each of the four large windows.

The strangest thing was the man and two women sitting on a chaise longue and thoroughly enjoying themselves. She gasped the moment she realized the man was gripping one woman's bare breast while enthusiastically kissing the other woman, who had just freed his hard cock from his tuxedo pants.

She turned and ran back into the hallway, ready to yell for the butler to appear with her coat so she could get the hell out of here. But her phone buzzed and she hustled to dig it out of her purse before it disturbed the threesome.

Come upstairs. First room to your left.

Riley read the text and her fingers immediately began moving over the screen.

I don't think so. There are people having sex in the front room.

She hit Send and looked around. It was relatively quiet considering what was happening in

that other room. Curiosity had Riley stepping ten-
tatively through the second door. This room had a
much lighter color scheme but Riley was beyond the
decor at this point. Another man dressed in a tuxedo
was standing against a wall, his head leaned back,
eyes closed, face contorted in desire as the woman
on her knees in front of him sucked his cock deep
into her mouth. Not six feet from them was a woman
wearing a gorgeous orange gown with a split high
up her right thigh. She was making use of that split
because one of her legs was draped over the arm of
the French armchair while her fingers toyed with
her exposed clit.

Riley's mouth clamped shut, not just because she
was shocked, but because of the flush that quickly
came over her skin. She felt warm and… She didn't
even want to admit it. Her phone buzzed again.

Come on up, Riley. I'm waiting for you.

She turned and walked slowly out of that room,
still trying to figure out what was happening. Without any clear answers Riley started up the stairs.

When you come in, close and lock the door and
then wait for me.

What the hell was this? And who did Chaz think
she was? Riley did not do games and she definitely
did not do sex games. She should leave right now

and let him play at whatever this was by himself. But she didn't. She walked up to the painted door and touched the bronze handle. Her hand stayed on the handle a few seconds longer than necessary as she stepped into the dimly lit room. The floor was carpeted, walls a rich mahogany filled with bookshelves and large gold-framed paintings. There were also a lot of chairs in this room. One in front of each of the three windows, a couch centered beneath a painting, two side chairs and two cherry-oak wood stools with brass legs. Across from all the chairs was an ornate bar, fully stocked.

Riley's heart beat faster, her breasts feeling a bit full from what she'd seen downstairs and her mind curious enough to have her closing the door and locking it.

"Now what?" She spoke into the room because she presumed that Chaz was here somewhere, but then she recalled his last text said for her to wait for him.

Take off your clothes.

That was the next message and Riley was already shaking her head.

"Not on your life, Chaz. If this is your idea of a date, it's no wonder you're still single."

There's nobody in this room but you and me. Take off your clothes.

Riley was about to type *no*. She was going to answer him and run down those stairs, find her coat and go home. Alone. To do what she did every night—work until she fell asleep and then get up in the morning and work some more. She held the phone in her palm and looked around. There were only two other doors in addition to the one she'd just come through. One was probably a bathroom and the other a closet, maybe.

It's just you and me?

She typed the reply, not totally sure where her mind was going.

Yes. I want you naked.

Riley read his words and her pussy throbbed.

She stood in that spot, hearing her heart pound like a drumbeat throughout the room. Chaz wanted her to do the things these other people in this house were doing. He hadn't asked her, they'd never discussed anything like sex parties or exhibitionism. She should feel offended that he would make this type of assumption about her. But she wasn't.

Riley was definitely aroused. She could picture herself sucking Chaz's dick just like that woman downstairs was doing. She'd done it before when they were in Milan and she wanted to do it again. Besides, there was no exhibitionism in this room, alone with him. Chaz obviously wanted to watch her get naked knowing there was a houseful of people. The thought had her pussy jumping again and her breath skipping as she contemplated what to do next.

I want YOU naked.

The response came to her mind quickly and she typed it before she could rethink it. Feeling emboldened she typed a quick follow-up.

Take off your clothes and come to me.

The room was silent and she moved to the coffee table to set her purse down. She rubbed her hands up and down her arms and wondered if he were just going to leave. The door across the room opened and Riley got her answer.

Chaz stepped through the door and he was gloriously naked. Riley had seen him that way before but this was different. It was on her command.

"What are you going to do with me now that I'm here?"

There was no hint of play in his tone or the way he was staring at her. There was only hunger and need, both so thick the room felt instantly full.

"You're not close enough," she said and watched him walk closer.

Every part of him was toned or muscled—his biceps, calves, abs, ass. She couldn't have sculpted a more perfect male body. Her fingers ached to touch him as he stopped just a few inches in front of her, but she refrained. Instead Riley walked around him, looking him up and down from head to toe.

"There's a scar here." She didn't touch that part of his lower back that snaked around his waist jaggedly. This one was longer than the scar beneath his pectoral. She'd felt and seen both before, but had never asked.

"Motorcycle accident when I was twenty."

She was in front of him again, noting that out-of-context question had done nothing to still the desire threatening to burn through her clothes.

"You didn't answer my question. What are you going to do with me, Riley?"

She only took a second to think before bending her knees and going to the floor. His dick was in her hand one moment, in her mouth the next. He was thick and heavy as her fingers stroked the inches her mouth did not cover. She loved the warm feel of him resting flat on her tongue. On a soft moan she sucked him in, holding him inside her warm mouth until she heard the wisp of breath come from between his lips.

He would try to hold on to control; that was the type of guy Chaz was. But not tonight. Tonight was for Riley. She was in control and she was going to get everything she wanted.

Riley moved her other hand to rub his balls while she sucked him in deeper. She increased her speed, pausing in intervals to drag her tongue up and down his length, dipping into his slit before sucking him inside once more. He tried to put a hand to the back of her head but she'd swatted it away before returning to massage his tightened sac. There was an urge inside her pushing her further, until she was making sounds and sucking him in a way she'd never known she could.

He groaned, cursed, whispered her name through clenched teeth and it made her even more determined to take everything she could from him in this moment. She needed this like she needed air. The power that was coursing through her veins was addictive, the heavy pounding of his dick in her mouth erotic as hell.

"I'm not gonna be able to stop."

His words were strained and in her mind she replied, *I don't want you to.*

Her mouth and tongue gave him the answer in another way, working over him until she could feel his legs tensing and heard the groan that seemed to come from somewhere deep inside him.

"Riley!"

His shout sounded painful just before the first spurt of his release hit the back of her throat. Riley closed her eyes and swallowed.

* * *

Chaz grasped Riley's shoulders and pulled her up to him. He moved his hands to her cheeks and lowered his mouth over hers. The kiss was no match for the way her mouth had just worked over his dick but he thrust his tongue deep inside, feeling hers and tasting himself.

The thumping in his head had to be the sound of his blood pumping thick and fast through his veins. It was loud and encouraging, pushing the desire he was already experiencing into full-blown passion. He needed more of her right now.

"Too many clothes," he groaned and pulled his mouth from hers long enough to lift her blouse from her skirt and pull it over her head. She pushed the skirt down her legs and he whispered, "Thank you. Thank you."

They worked together to remove her boots and underwear, and when she was thankfully naked, Chaz picked her up and sat her in one of the side chairs.

"Thought about you all day," he mumbled as he lifted her legs and placed each one over the arm of the chair.

She opened like a beautiful flower, her swollen labia coated with the thick gloss of her essence.

He glanced up to see that she was staring at him intently. "Is all that for me?"

"Only if you want it."

He should have known her reply would not be a submission. Still, it was sexy as hell.

Chaz grinned at her seconds before going in. He touched his tongue directly to her opening and she hissed. Her hands went to the back of his head but he followed her previous lead and pushed them away. From that moment on she was his, whether she wanted to admit it or not. Every sound she whimpered, every thrust of her hips and finally the sweet feel of her coming for him sealed the deal.

But it still wasn't enough.

He stood, hating to leave the sweetness of her, and picked up one of the condoms he'd left on the coffee table.

"I thought this would be over by now," he said when his hand was moving over his length, smoothing the latex in place. "It wasn't supposed to last this long."

She'd been staring at his dick and now she reluctantly dragged her gaze up to his. She licked her lips and stood from the chair. "I know."

Her brown nipples were hard and puckered against the creamy hue of her skin. Her waist was small but the curve of her hips and ass was generous.

"I can't stop wanting you," he admitted.

She looked like she might say something in opposition but whispered, "I can't stop wanting you, either."

Relief, desire, need, hunger all washed over Chaz

in the seconds after she said those words. It wasn't a declaration of love, which he was definitely not looking for, but it was better. She wanted as badly as he did and neither of them could explain why.

He went to her and cupped his hands at her waist before hoisting her up. She wrapped her legs around his waist, clasping her ankles at his back. Chaz speared into her and she moaned. He pumped in and out of her until she was bouncing over his dick, her arms wrapped around his neck as her back arched. Penetration was deep and felt like heaven.

He held her in his arms, easing in and out of her with his eyes wide-open so he could see passion and pleasure streak over her face. Riley was a lovely woman, but in the throes of passion she was absolutely gorgeous. He loved every sound she made, every time she pulled her lip between her teeth and the simple flare of her nostrils as she struggled to breathe. Everything, including the tight clench of her walls around his dick, Chaz loved it all. And he had no idea what he was going to do when it was over.

He closed his eyes to that thought and pumped faster until his release was pulsing into the condom and she was quivering in his grasp.

It was over. For now, he reminded himself.

The night was still young and Riley was still down for this affair. Chaz refused to think about that any further.

She fell forward, laying her head on his shoulder and snuggling closer to him. Chaz's legs wobbled slightly after the force of his climax, but he held on to her. Wrapping one arm even tighter around her back, while the other went lower so that his hand cupped her ass.

He wasn't letting go…not tonight.

CHAPTER FIFTEEN

"IT'S BETTER IF we switch it up," Riley said. "We don't want anyone to see you at my building too many times."

Because they were having a secret affair. Riley didn't have to speak those words. Chaz had been replaying them in his mind on the drive from the house in Lennox Hill to his 92nd Street apartment an hour and a half later.

"Don't you agree?"

"Ah, yeah. That's a good point." It made sense. That didn't mean he had to like it. But when exactly did he stop liking the agreement they'd made?

"I thought you were inviting me to dinner. I'm starving."

Chaz unlocked the door and waited for her to enter ahead of him. "We can order something."

Because he definitely planned for her to stay the night.

"I'm in the mood for pizza."

He took the coat she shrugged out of and turned to hang it in the coat closet. "You eat pizza?"

She made a face—not exactly a frown and not a smile. "Who doesn't eat pizza?"

She was right. It was silly of him to think that the infamous Riley Gold didn't eat pizza. She was just so different from the type of woman he'd thought she was. In fact, everything he'd learned about Riley in the past weeks had been contrary to what he'd thought about her for years.

"I like everything on mine. How do you take yours?"

They were walking deeper into the living room and Chaz moved his hand over the wall switch to turn on the recessed lights in the ceiling. In stark contrast to Riley's cool, contemporary decor, Chaz favored warm, dark colors and minimal furniture. She stood on the cobalt blue rug and looked around at the blue Bradford sofa, matching side chairs and marble coffee table.

"Anything as long as there's lots of cheese." She didn't look at him as she spoke but continued assessing the room. "You like blue and open windows."

Chaz also had a wall of windows in the living room. His actually stretched up to the second floor. On the lower level there were no blinds, so the city was as much a part of this space as the furniture and the sleek fireplace on the wall behind him. Upstairs he did have remote blinds similar to hers but he rarely closed the blinds. Tonight he would make an exception.

"I'll order two pizzas and fries. I like fries with my pizza." He pulled his phone out of his pocket. "And yes, blue is my favorite color. What's yours?"

Chaz scrolled through his saved numbers. There were only a few things in his cooking repertoire so he knew all the best places to order food.

"Wine. The color, not the drink."

She sat on the couch and Chaz admired the soft pink of her blouse against the bold blue hue. He also loved the way the material of her skirt moved with her body, easing up her thigh as she sat back on the chair and crossed one leg over the other.

"That's an interesting color." For a very interesting woman.

When the food was ordered and Chaz had ditched the suit jacket and tie he'd worn to the party, he fixed them both a drink. They needed it. Especially since he knew he wasn't going to escape without Riley asking why he'd invited her to that party. He didn't have long to wait.

She took a tentative sip from her glass and then looked over at him. Chaz had taken a seat on the couch beside her, because there was no way he was sitting across the room from her. Pretenses between them were unnecessary.

"Are sex parties your thing?"

She lifted one elegantly arched brow with the

question and he tried to decipher if she was just curious or whether she was judging him. Considering Riley's past, he went with curiosity.

"They're entertaining. And no, not because I like to have sex with multiple people or in front of people. Not that I think there's anything wrong with either lifestyle. For me, it's about atmosphere and sensory reactions."

She shook her head and shrugged. "I don't follow. You either go to sex parties for sex or you don't."

"Life's not black-and-white, Riley. I know you believe in good and bad, right and wrong, but I've always lived in the gray area."

Chaz leaned forward and rested his elbows on his knees. This wasn't a conversation he'd ever had to indulge in before, but he wanted her to know. He wanted to see her reaction to the real Chadwick Warren.

"My uncle gets married and divorced every time the wind changes. Or so it seems. My parents had a committed and long-lasting relationship full of love and respect. I'm somewhere in between. I don't do love, but I love sex. So I go to parties and surround myself with people who love sex."

"You're the hottest social media bachelor in the world. I read that in the *Wall Street Journal*. Your net worth is somewhere around twenty-three billion. You could have any woman you wanted—one who's well-versed in the sex-without-commitment games—

in your bed every night. Why would you need to go to a sex party?"

"No judgment. No recriminations. No questions. Half the time nobody even knows who I am for that matter. And believe it or not, I've only ever had sex at a party three times. Each time I brought the woman with me and asked if she were comfortable indulging. You are certainly blunt, Riley."

"If we're talking about this we might as well talk honestly, right?"

He nodded. "Yeah. You're right."

She'd worn her hair down tonight, falling past her shoulders in a tumble of waves. It was a softer look than she normally displayed in public. He liked it.

"Sometimes I need to get away from the world I've created for myself. The world where they expect me to be the famous social media bachelor or billionaire entrepreneur. I'm not Tobias's orphaned nephew. I'm just Chaz, a man who likes and knows pleasure." It sounded so simple to him but he wondered what she thought about what she was hearing.

"Did you like being there?" he asked.

"I've never been to a sex party before."

"I figured as much. My question was did you like it?"

She ran her palms down her thighs and cleared her throat. "Yes. I think I did. Not at first. When I walked into that room and saw that threesome, I wanted to curse you from here to hell and back for inviting me to such a place. But then I saw a man receiving his pleasure and a woman giving herself pleasure and I was…aroused. Never in a million years would I have thought something like that would turn me on."

"You're a passionate woman, Riley. You shouldn't be ashamed of that."

"I'm not ashamed of anything," she countered.

But that wasn't true. She was ashamed of their affair. Or she was afraid of anyone finding out about it. Either way, Chaz didn't like it and he wondered how she was going to react when he finally told her his feelings about their arrangement had changed.

"Thank you for the vase."

It was just before dawn. The sky was that amazing mixture of orange and pink, and she could see daylight peeking through the pale gray shades Chaz had lowered over the twenty-foot windows in his bedroom. The forest-green-and-white-striped comforter on his bed was warm even if it wasn't something she would have purchased. But what Riley really liked about being in Chaz's bed early on a Saturday morning was the feel of his strong arms wrapped around her, the warmth of his body against hers and the press of his heavy arousal against her ass.

"You're welcome." His breath was warm against the back of her neck. "I figured it would be nice if you had something calming to look at while you're in the office. A dildo slash paperweight wouldn't go over very well."

She smiled, something she'd been doing a lot of lately, especially when she was with him.

"That was very thoughtful. I didn't expect that from you."

"Why? Because we're only having an affair?"

Riley frowned, hating the way he said that word. Why? It was what they'd agreed on.

"Because you're not what I expected."

"You expected the billionaire bachelor who would sleep with you a couple times and move on?"

"Yes." His words were exactly right. "But I think I also expected you to be sneaky and conniving like your uncle."

"My uncle is neither of those things, and besides that, I'm not him. And we're not that feud. Didn't we already talk about this?"

"We did and you're right. We're not the feud but we're not absolved of it, either. The remnants of your uncle stealing designs from the fashion house my grandfather started that allowed Tobias to get his start affect us whether we want it to or not."

"What are you talking about? My uncle said the feud started over a woman and even when Ron had gotten the girl he'd still been horribly jealous and forced Uncle Tobias out of the company."

She'd never heard the story that way before and didn't really know if she believed it, but the fact still remained that there was definite animosity between their families and that was likely to always create friction between them.

They remained silent for the next few minutes, until she couldn't stand it any longer.

"I like being with you. I didn't think I would, but I do." There, she'd said what had been on her mind all night. Or rather the times that he wasn't inside her and she wasn't asleep.

"I knew I would like being with you," he said. "Just not this much."

His lips touched the back of her shoulder and warmth flooded her body. Why was it like that with him? It shouldn't have felt right and she shouldn't have wanted it to feel this way all the time. This couldn't be happening. Not to her and definitely not with him.

"Shower with me." She said the words and sat straight up in bed before she talked herself out of it.

When he didn't answer, Riley looked back over her shoulder. "Take a shower with me, Chaz, and then I'll fix us breakfast."

"Music to my ears!" He jumped out of the bed.

Riley chuckled and pushed the covers back. She was about to get off the bed and walk to the bathroom but Chaz scooped her up into his arms and carried her naked body. He was naked, too, so once they were in the bathroom and he set her down, Riley reached for him. She laced her arms around his neck and drew his mouth to hers for a soft kiss.

His tongue was warm against hers, soothing her immediately. Riley didn't need soothing from frayed nerves or even the fear of falling headlong into an anxiety attack, not this time. Instead she had questions that she'd never imagined having, and Chaz was the only one who could answer them.

The kiss was doing the trick. The way his tongue leisurely stroked hers and his lips slanted over hers should have started the inevitable sexual arousal. It didn't. Not this time. Instead it made Riley lean in closer and ease her arms around his waist. The urge to hold on to him was strong. The need to feel him gripping her in the same way was deep.

His arms moved around her waist, his palms flat against her skin in what Riley would swear was a tender embrace instead of a heated one. Not that she minded the heat—this morning she just craved something more.

Chaz broke the kiss. He pulled his mouth away from hers but stared down at her for endless moments. She couldn't look away from him. Not from his smoldering eyes or the thin line of his lips. When he brushed his knuckles over her jaw, she wanted to sigh. He dropped his hand abruptly and moved to the shower to turn on the water.

Riley stepped inside when he just stood by the glass doors. His shower was larger than hers.

Probably because he didn't have a tub in his bathroom and she'd insisted on a soaker tub and a large shower. The water was closer to being hot than warm, just the way she liked it, and Riley immediately stepped beneath the spray. She turned and tilted her head back, drenching her hair. Her eyes were closed so she didn't see Chaz come to stand beside her but she did hear the click of the shower stall door closing. Then his hands were in her hair, running his fingers through the thick mass just like the water.

"Oh, guess I should have asked first—do you have a shampoo with conditioner?"

He reached behind himself into an alcove in the gray tiled wall and brought a white bottle up to her face.

"Will this work?"

Of course, it wasn't her brand. She'd never found herself washing her hair without her own products, but she'd also never showered with a man before. Riley shrugged and reached for the bottle.

Chaz held it back from her. "I'll do it."

She was going to question him because she felt a trickle of fear at how serious and at the same time how wonderfully intimate this felt, but she couldn't find the words. Instead she stood there and waited while he squeezed shampoo into his hand and then put the bottle back on the shelf.

"My hair's really thick so you might need a little more," she said, then clamped her mouth shut.

His hands were already in her hair, moving until he'd built up a lather. Then he was raking his fingertips over her scalp, massaging and raking, rotating until Riley could no longer hold back her moan.

"That feels fantastic." And she wasn't even exaggerating. It almost felt sensual in a clean sort of way. She couldn't actually explain it, just knew that it was a feeling she thoroughly enjoyed.

When he was finished massaging her scalp until Riley thought she might curl up on the shower floor and fall asleep, Chaz eased her back under the spray and rinsed her hair clean. Riley reached into that same alcove and pulled out the bottle of body wash. There was a cloth on the shelf as well, and she filled it with body wash before replacing the bottle.

She touched it to his chest first, watching the big frothy bubbles cover the toned pectorals and move down his sculpted abs. She washed his whole body, wondering if he was experiencing the slow burning warmth spreading throughout like she was. After he rinsed, Chaz returned the favor and before long the shower was over. Chaz turned off the water, but they did not move. They stood in the center of the shower stall, water dripping from their bodies, and simply stared at each other. As if really seeing each other for the first time.

It was in that moment that Riley knew. It had come to her sometime during the night—this crazy idea that she and Chaz could be like this for real, in public and in private, for a very long time.

It had come to her and now she worried there was no turning back.

CHAPTER SIXTEEN

ON MONDAY MORNING Riley rode in the back of the town car with Chaz. The windows were tinted and the driver, the man she'd seen driving Chaz many times before, stared straight ahead as usual. Riley wondered if he knew who she was and, if so, why he hadn't leaked to the press how many times he'd seen her and Chaz together. It was a sobering thought, especially since she'd spent the entire weekend in Chaz's apartment not thinking of their affair as a secret at all. In the privacy of his home they'd been free from any scrutiny or recriminations, something she was certain they both enjoyed.

"This week is going to be hectic for me," Chaz said. "I'm sure your schedule is similar."

She ran a hand down the leg of her pants. When it seemed apparent that she would be spending the weekend with Chaz, they'd taken a quick trip to her penthouse to grab some clothes. Still, they'd decided it was best for her to abide by her normal workday routine and drive her own car from her building garage to work.

"Definitely," she replied. "Our show is Sunday and there's still so much to do. We have the media brunch on Saturday and from what I heard parts of the show are still being choreographed."

"I had no idea how much work went into these shows," Chaz continued. "We had a situation at the rehearsal on Friday that I'm sure I'll have to deal with this morning."

"Really? I hope it wasn't anything that'll affect your show." Riley meant those words.

King Designs was a great fashion house that produced quality work. She could admit that regardless of what happened between her father and Tobias. And to be quite honest, she was anxious to see their collection this season, especially since this was the first time Chaz had been actively involved in the business.

"I'm not sure." His words and the pensive look on his face said he was truly worried about whatever had happened.

"There's always something at the last minute. Some glitch with the technical plans for a show or, more serious, an issue with a design. If things ever went too smoothly we'd probably all need to be concerned. But I'm sure it'll work out."

She reached for his hand and squeezed. When

he looked at her and smiled, Riley felt the familiar warmth they shared.

"I'm sure your new collection is going to be a big hit. Your family will be impressed, and the press will have no choice but to give you the respect you've earned."

Riley smiled and let that bit of validation settle over her comfortably. His confidence in her had never wavered and because of that she believed his words.

"I know I didn't design the gowns but I feel like this entire collection is mine. I've worked so closely with the designers and production team to bring this new vision into fruition. Usually I'm all about my numbers and reports but this time I actually had the opportunity to put all my research into a product that RGF can be proud of."

Chaz lifted her hand to his lips and kissed her knuckles. "You're good at what you do, Riley. I know that and I'm not even as ensconced in this industry as you are. And you're passionate about your work. That's what really counts."

"You're not passionate about the fashion industry, are you?" Riley wondered if once Fashion Week was over, Chaz would return to Miami and to his media corporation.

He shrugged. "I've sort of been on the outskirts of the industry all my life. Living in that gray area I like." He grinned and Riley thought how liberating it must be to create a safe space to live and not give a damn what anyone thought about it.

"But I have to admit using my skills to create a brand that best represents my uncle and his vision for the company has been fun. I mean, I never actually thought I had a place at King Designs because it wasn't like my father had built that company. I figured I'd have to make my own place in this world and I have. I love what I've built at Conversation Media and I'd never totally walk away from that. Speaking of which, the new app is launching on Thursday, the day before our show."

"Oh, wow, you really do have a big week. Well, I just might download the ChatMe app to see what it's all about."

"It's not a dating app." He said those words quickly. "Not that you would ever need an app to help find a date."

"No," she replied, a bit more sober now than she'd been just a few seconds ago. "I don't usually think much about dating."

They fell silent and Chaz ran his thumb over the back of her hand.

"We've been having a good time, haven't we?"

She nodded. "Yes. We have. I didn't really know what to expect, but yeah, this has been fun."

"Fun enough to keep going? I mean, to continue seeing each other?"

Hadn't this been what Riley thought about all weekend?

"I'd like that." The words slipped easily from her lips just as the car pulled up in front of her building. She looked out the window and then back to Chaz.

He leaned over and touched his lips lightly to hers.

"I know you have to go. The talented Riley Gold has to be great this week. And I, the outsider, have a lot to do, as well. So we'll talk about this after we've both survived Fashion Week."

His voice was a deep whisper against her lips and Riley eased in for another kiss. "Yes, we'll definitely talk about this when this week is over."

Their next kiss was longer, slower and sweeter than Riley had ever experienced. She loved it and did not want it to end.

"I'll call you later," he said when they pulled apart.

Riley smiled. "Or I'll call you."

Chaz grinned and in the next second the driver was opening the door for her.

Twelve hours later a tired but invigorated Riley pulled into the garage and parked her car before taking the elevator up to the penthouse. Her stomach growled as she walked through the door and Riley immediately thought about ordering a pizza. It was a little after eight in the evening and she hadn't eaten since a tuna sandwich at two in the afternoon. She knew there was something in her freezer that she could just pop into the microwave, but she wanted pizza with everything on it and fries.

She wanted that connection to Chaz.

Speaking of which, once she was in her bedroom and had kicked off her heels, Riley reached into her purse for her phone. No call or text from Chaz, not since earlier in the day when he'd checked to see if she'd eaten lunch, which she'd dutifully ordered as soon as she hung up with him. Her afternoon had been swamped and she figured his had been, too, so she sent a quick text.

Thinking about you.

It was honest and sincere and the first time she'd ever said such a thing to a man. Riley smiled with how good it made her feel. She was about to grab some pajamas and head into the bathroom for a shower when her doorbell rang. A giddy flutter whirled through her stomach as she hoped it was Chaz surprising her with dinner and company for the evening. Her penthouse suddenly seemed too big for just her and definitely too quiet. But when Riley walked back into the living room and excitedly pulled the door open, her happiness faded fast.

"Hey, Dad. RJ. Come on in."

"We need to talk." Her father's tone was brisk as he removed his coat and walked into the living room.

RJ followed Ron inside. His expression was somber, his tone grave as he said, "Hey."

She closed the door and followed them inside.

"What's up? Did something happen during rehearsal? Is there a problem with one of the gowns?"

RGF was presenting a record forty-two designs during this show. Ten of them were from Riley's bridal collection.

"Yes," Ron replied tightly.

"Sort of," RJ added.

Riley looked from her father to her brother and back to her father again. "Just tell me what happened." Because she was certain something very bad was about to go down.

She could see it in the lines on her father's forehead and the muscle pulsing in RJ's jaw.

"Why don't we start with you telling us where the hell you were this weekend?" If she hadn't been certain before, her father's tone conveyed every bit of the anger he was feeling.

Riley squared her shoulders and looked him directly in the eye. "I'm an adult, Dad. I don't have to explain where I was or why without knowing the reason for the request."

It was a bold statement to make to a man like Ron Gold but Riley didn't care. She didn't like her father and brother coming into her house at this time of night, questioning her and staring at her as if she'd done something wrong.

"If you would just tell me what's going on—"

"What's going on with you and Chaz Warren? Why were you photographed getting out of a limousine with him and going into his apartment building? And this morning you were dropped off here by a car registered to King Designs."

The vein in her father's head that only popped out when he was seething with rage was throbbing front and center, and Riley's fingers clenched at her sides. RJ had folded his arms over his chest in what she knew was his authoritative stance.

"I have a right to a personal life" was all Riley would say.

"With him?" RJ asked. "You know the story and you know how this looks."

"I know who makes me feel good," she snapped. "And what, are you two having me followed? Is that what we do now? Follow Riley around to make sure she doesn't mess up again?"

"But you have messed up," Ron countered. "Because not only are you sleeping with the enemy, but the enemy is stabbing you in the back as expected."

"What are you talking about?"

"That editor I know at that little tabloid—he called me an hour ago to give me a heads-up."

That giddy feeling Riley had felt in her stomach just a few short moments ago was now a heated ball of dread.

"A heads-up about what?" She said the words slowly, as if she didn't really want the answer.

"Not only are the pictures of you and Chaz going to be printed in tomorrow's paper but they're attached to a sneak peek at King's new collection. A wedding gown, Riley. And it looks very similar to one of ours," RJ said.

"Not similar," her father roared. "It's the exact same gown! They copied our gown and are offering a sneak peek before the shows so it'll look like we're the ones who copied them. Chaz Warren is behind this! He probably stole the sketch while you were sleeping in his bed."

Riley felt hot all over. Her arms began to shake and for just a second her vision blurred. This could not be happening. Not again.

RJ stepped closer to her. "What did you tell him, Riley? Did you show him the sketches?"

"No!" She could not have said the word more vehemently. "I would never do such a thing." And Chaz would never ask her something like that.

"You bring work home with you all the time. Was he here? Could you have left him alone with sensitive information? It would have only taken a second. Just like his uncle, dammit!" Her father persisted.

"He is not like his uncle!" The minute the words were out Riley realized her mistake. She saw the concern on RJ's face and unabashed fury on her father's.

She turned away and walked toward the window. Tears stung her eyes. They wanted to fall but Riley wouldn't let them. She almost folded her arms over her chest, to cradle herself and hopefully bring some comfort to the deep slice of hurt that had been opened in her. But she didn't. Instead she took deep breaths. She was way too upset for the breaths to be slow, as she'd been taught to do when threatened with an anxiety attack, but at least she was breathing. Her hands were shaking and she finally gave in and clasped her fingers together in front of her.

"Riley."

RJ was right behind her and she prayed he wouldn't touch her. After the breakup with Walt her family had rallied around her, each of them hugging her and consoling her to the point that all Riley had done for days was cry over a man she'd never loved. Tonight, the tears that burned were for a man she'd just begun to believe she could love. And she was an idiot for giving in to the dream.

"I never left any sensitive materials around him, even though I never believed he was with me just to steal our ideas." Saying the words aloud meant something. Riley just couldn't figure out what, not right now, when the pain was so raw.

"That's how they work. They befriend you and then they stab you in the back. You should have known better. You should have kept a closer eye on him."

Riley swung around. "You were friends with Tobias King for thirty-four years. The two of you worked side by side at your father's company. You didn't just leave sensitive information around him, you shared a business with him. So don't lecture me about what I should have done differently."

RJ touched a hand to her shoulder and Riley shrugged it away.

"I don't know how they got the information. Maybe the reporter is making this up." She needed to believe there was another explanation.

RJ came close again, this time putting his phone in front of her.

"Here are the pictures of you and Chaz together." He swiped left. "And these are the pictures of the gown."

Her chest caved with dread but Riley held it together. She swiped to the right to see the pictures of her and Chaz. It was Friday night when they'd left the party in Lennox Hill. They'd dressed quickly after their tryst and Chaz had suggested they go to his place. He was holding her hand as they walked to the curb to wait for the limo he'd reserved. She could still remember the warmth of his touch and how close he'd sat to her in the back of the limo. Swiping to the next picture, she cringed because it was just as her father had stated: this morning when she'd gotten out of Chaz's car in front of her building.

"Who would have been following us?" She looked

up at RJ. "We hadn't been at a fashion event and we were far away from either of our offices, so somebody must have intentionally followed us."

Ron frowned. "Yes, that's something I absolutely will not tolerate. We have to get ahead of this. I'll contact the police just to get a complaint started. Also, my guy's agreed to run the picture of our gown at the same time as the King gown."

"No!" Riley shook her head. "We don't give in to the press. We don't let them get the upper hand. Isn't that what you've always told me?"

"I also told you not to give them ammunition, Riley. Now we don't have a choice but to play this hand all the way." Ron looked at RJ.

"Send the picture to him tonight and we're pulling that gown from the show. Make it known that we're outraged at Tobias's duplicity and that we don't feel King Designs is in any way a threat to us." Her father spoke in absolute terms so that RJ only nodded.

"But we're doing the exact opposite. If we're so sure they're no competition to us why not show our entire collection on Sunday as planned? So what if theirs is hitting the papers tomorrow? You don't think people will see the difference and know which is the better product? You don't trust your clientele?"

"I don't trust Tobias King or his nephew," Ron told her. "And you shouldn't, either. Whatever you were doing with Chaz Warren, you should stop it now. He's only interested in you because you're my daughter."

All the air left Riley's lungs and she felt light-headed. She rubbed a hand down the back of her neck and sighed. "I need to be alone."

"Let's just meet tomorrow," RJ said when Ron looked as if he was going to say something else. "Be in the office at seven."

"Fine," Riley snapped and walked to the door to see them out.

RJ followed her, then leaned in and kissed her on the forehead. "It's going to be all right."

Riley closed her eyes and accepted her brother's words. He loved her and wanted what was best for her—he just didn't know what that was. And for the record, at this point, neither did Riley.

Ron stepped up to her, looking at her with his big brown eyes, his mouth bent into a frown just before he pulled her into a hug. Riley had to fight every instinct she had. How many times had she cried in his arms when she was a little girl? But Riley wasn't that girl anymore and she'd cried enough.

"I'll see you in the morning," she said when he pulled away because she couldn't say anything else.

After the breakup with Walt she'd apologized to her parents and brothers profusely for how she'd messed up. Tonight, she couldn't say those words. She'd trusted and she'd believed and a part of her knew she wasn't wrong for doing either of those things. The other part… Well, once she closed and locked the door, Riley fell back against it. She closed her eyes and whispered, "Oh, Chaz, what have you done?"

CHAPTER SEVENTEEN

IT WAS EIGHT THIRTY in the morning when Chaz walked into his office at King Designs. He felt like he'd just left this place and now he was back again.

Yesterday had been hectic with Tobias calling Chaz into a meeting with Lenzo fifteen minutes after Chaz had arrived at the office. Chaz was still riding on the high of the weekend with Riley until he'd stood in a room with a designer who apparently hated him.

"He's not a designer. You brought him in because he's your relative, not because he has an ounce of experience in this industry. And then you expect me to stand on my head to please him. Hell no, Tobias! I've been with you for ten years and this is how you treat me!"

Lenzo's fists were clenched at his sides while Chaz stood next to his uncle's desk.

"This is my company, Lenzo. I call the shots. Whether you like my calls or not. And if you had a problem with Chaz you should have come to me and perhaps we could have worked it out. But as it stands now I'm letting you go."

"You're what?" Lenzo's eyes almost bulged from his face. "You're firing me because I wouldn't listen to this playboy's advice?"

Chaz had been called worse than a playboy.

"It's not about my advice," he'd said. "You were instructed six months ago to follow my rebranding plan. You chose not to do that."

"Security will escort you out," Tobias told him.

When that scene was over, Chaz had returned to his office, where one issue after another plagued him, including a press sheet he received from his marketing team about ChatMe. Juggling two major business events in one week wasn't the smartest plan, but he was determined to make it all work. Before long the day and night had gotten away from him. Chaz didn't get a moment to look at his phone until he'd walked into his apartment at a little after midnight.

Riley's message immediately warmed him and he'd smiled.

Missed you so much today.

He'd typed his response seconds before falling face-first onto his bed and into a deep slumber.

Now he checked his phone for the fourth time since leaving his apartment this morning. There was no response from Riley.

After dropping his briefcase onto the floor beside his desk, Chaz plugged his phone into the charger and set it near his laptop. Easing down into his chair, he tried to focus on what he needed to tackle first. He definitely wanted to go over the press sheet for the ChatMe launch one more time. Valeria wasn't publishing his interview on her blog, nor was there going to be any type of advertising on her YouTube show. He chuckled at how petty she was being but decided to move on.

His fingers moved quickly over the keyboard as he pulled up his Conversation Media account. He was about to send a message to his team when the door to his office opened.

"What the hell is this?" Tobias stormed into the office.

He dropped not one but three tabloid papers onto Chaz's desk.

"What were you thinking? We never, *ever* allow items from our collection to be photographed and printed before the show!"

The look on Tobias's face, his tone and the head-lines on the tabloids all brought Chaz to a full stop.

"First, I never gave permission for anything to be printed." Especially not the pictures of him and Riley, which were staring back at him in full color.

Tobias didn't seem to hear a word he said as his rant continued. "And you're sleeping with Ron's daughter? I told you to watch out for that one and you jump into bed with her? What the hell is wrong with you?"

Chaz stood and looked his uncle in the eye. "I did not approve any of these pictures and who I sleep with is my business. Always has been and always will be."

"She's the enemy's daughter!"

"She's *your* enemy's daughter. To me she's just a woman that I lo—have grown very fond of in the past weeks. And I don't appreciate someone following us around and printing malicious lies about us." Chaz really had no idea what the articles said. All he knew was that there were pictures of him and Riley and that was enough.

Tobias pointed at the picture of a dress. "This dress right here is one of the ones you pulled from the show. How did someone get it? Was it Riley? Did you show her our collection?"

Chaz looked closer at the papers. He lined them up next to each other and stared at the pictures, thinking. "We said no bridal couture this season. That's why I took the dress out of the show."

"I know that! What I'm asking is how Riley knew."

Chaz glanced up at his uncle. "What would she gain by releasing our dress to the press early? Not that I'm saying she's responsible." Because she wasn't. Chaz was certain of that fact. He was also positive that the moment Riley saw these papers she was going to totally lose it.

"Well, somebody leaked the picture. And do you see Ron's pompous remarks? He's not at all threatened by whatever we have in our show. To hell with him and his king-of-the-world attitude!"

Chaz grabbed his phone and was headed toward the door when Tobias called to him.

"Where are you going? We've got to deal with this!"

"I've got something else to deal with first."

Tobias sighed heavily. "She is not the priority, Chaz. She's the enemy."

Chaz stopped at the door. He turned around and remembered all the things his uncle had done for him. All the money he'd spent on his education and the time he'd taken teaching Chaz everything he needed to know about being a black man in this world. Chaz appreciated all of it and he loved Tobias, but today he was going to set him straight.

"I don't care what you think about Riley, or her family for that matter. But she means a lot to me and there's nothing you, this fashion house or anybody else can do to change that."

He walked out, not giving Tobias a moment to respond. Chaz didn't care what his response would have been. All he was concerned with right now was getting to Riley before she could see these papers.

"You didn't give them the picture like Dad told you to," Riley said to RJ.

She was sitting in her office and RJ was standing on the other side of her desk. Maurice was sitting in one of the guest chairs and Major leaned on the edge of her desk. They'd all filed into her office at seven this morning, tabloids in hand. Riley had already read the stories. She'd looked at the pictures again and she'd taken aspirin to ward off the headache that still pounded at her temples.

"You were right—it made it look as if we were conceding and we'd never do that. Dad's just working on anger right now, Ri. You know he didn't mean all that stuff he said to you last night." RJ could be the voice of reason where their father was concerned.

Riley didn't know if that was because he was the firstborn or because he was the one who would eventually take Ron's place at the helm. Either way, it annoyed Riley sometimes. Last night it had pissed her off.

"But let's clarify something," Maurice said. "You are sleeping with Chaz Warren?"

There were moments when Riley detested being the only girl among her siblings. This was definitely one of those moments. Having a sister here to help take some of the heat would have been fantastic. As it was, Riley would stand on her own, just like always.

"Yes. We met up in Milan and continued the affair here." She stopped before explaining any more because she'd said enough. In her mind, however, every second of her time with Chaz had been on replay.

She'd spent the whole night lying on her bed and trying to figure out when and where Chaz had stolen their design.

"And that's why you were acting different," RJ said.

"Different how? Please don't tell me she's fallen in love again," Maurice groaned and made a face.

If Riley weren't still very irritated she would have thrown something at her forever-juvenile brother.

"To be clear, I've never been in love," she stated.

"Because you've got good sense like the smart twin," Major added.

"Where's Dad? I thought he'd want to be here to continue his reprimand." And if her brothers were finished staring at her and questioning her, Riley would really like to get back to work.

"He wasn't here when I came in, so I figured we'd see him later," RJ said.

"That's not like him to miss an opportunity to rant about Tobias King," Major said. "Speaking of which, I've gotta say this was a pretty underhanded stunt and one Tobias could have certainly pulled a long time ago. Why now? Why this line and why target Riley again?"

Riley hadn't thought of those particular questions last night or this morning. She'd been too busy thinking about Chaz.

"Those are good questions," RJ stated just before the door to Riley's office was pushed open.

Chaz came in with Korey hot on his heels.

"I tried to tell him he wasn't welcome, but he pushed right past me!" Korey practically screamed those words the moment he made it into the office.

Chaz ignored him. "Riley, I need to talk to you."

Maurice bolted up from the chair and Major eased away from the desk. The twins fell in behind RJ, who immediately stepped up to face Chaz.

"That's not a good idea," RJ told him. "Neither was you coming here. You can turn around and leave now."

"I can call security," Korey added.

"I just want to speak to Riley. I'll leave as soon as I'm done," Chaz said evenly.

RJ wasn't budging. "You'll leave now."

Chaz shook his head. "No. Not until I talk to Riley."

Korey reached across Riley's desk to grab the phone. "I'm calling security!"

She stood and snatched the phone out of his hand and slammed it down.

"You are not calling anybody and I'm perfectly capable of deciding whether or not I want to talk to someone." She walked around her desk and pushed through the barrier the twins created with their matching muscular frames.

RJ didn't move so Riley walked around him. She felt utterly foolish stepping between him and Chaz, but it had to be done or the testosterone oozing in the room would reach a boiling point and all hell would definitely break loose.

"I don't think talking is necessary," she said when she finally looked up at Chaz.

"You're wrong. It's very necessary."

"Don't talk to my sister like that," Maurice snapped.

Riley figured this situation could only get worse, so she turned to face her brothers. "I've got this," she told them. "Leave us alone."

"Oh, hell no," Major chimed. "Leave him alone with you in your office?"

"I'll be fine," Riley told them, and while she was certain her brothers were concerned for her well-being, she had a suspicion they were also concerned about Chaz being in the office and possibly stealing more of their secrets.

"Really, you can all go now. This is my office."

RJ continued to glare at Chaz.

"You and I are going to have a conversation," he told Chaz.

Chaz nodded. "That's fine with me."

Her brothers filed out of the office and Chaz stared at Riley.

Riley turned to Korey, who was still leaning against the edge of her desk. "I'll be fine, Korey. You can leave us alone."

Korey looked at her another moment before pushing away from her desk. He did that thing with his fingers pointing to his eyes and then pointing to Chaz as he passed them and walked out.

When the door closed, Riley squared her shoulders and took a deep breath. She released it slowly before saying, "What do you want to say?"

He remained still.

"First, above all else I want to tell you that I've fallen in love with you, Riley Gold. I didn't mean to and I don't know exactly when it happened, but that's that."

Her hands were shaking and she hated it. She refused to clench her fingers or cross her arms or anything like that. She was going to face him and what he'd done head-on.

"Did you steal the design?"

Chaz flinched as if she'd hit him.

"No. I would never do anything to hurt you or your company. But I think I know how it might have happened."

"I don't want to do this, Chaz. I never wanted to do this. We were supposed to have an affair. Twenty-four hours and it was supposed to be over. If we'd just stuck to that none of this would have happened."

"None of this would have happened if someone hadn't copied your design and called it King's. Nothing you or I did led to this."

His tone was serious and his voice still rubbed her in that same sensual way. Riley hated that but couldn't change what was. Instead she turned away from him. She walked back to her desk because that was where she felt safest. At her desk everything was about work, about this company and their reputation. Standing too close to Chaz when he was saying those words… It was just too much.

"I'm not going to keep saying I didn't do this because I'd like to believe that you trust me enough to know better. Or that you have a modicum of respect for me after all we've shared."

She stopped on the other side of her desk but did not sit.

"You want to talk about respect, Chaz? Just how much respect do you think I'll get in this company now? My father thinks I'm too dense to know when a man I'm sleeping with steals from me. My brothers have already planned to hover over me for all the days of my life. And now, even my assistant is going to be giving me the side-eye because I agreed to talk to you." Her headache was pounding with full force now and Riley wanted desperately to go home, close her blinds and just sit in the dark for a while. There she only had to listen to her own voice telling her how foolish she'd been.

"So you really think I'd do that to you." It wasn't a question, just a somber statement.

Riley massaged her temples. "No," she said on a weary sigh. "I don't. And that makes this even more confusing."

"It doesn't have to be, Riley. We both know what we've shared and I have an idea of what's really going on with those pictures. So just let me figure it out and you continue to work on your show."

He'd come closer so that he stood right beside her now, but he didn't touch her. He wouldn't, not until she acted as if she were receptive to his touch. She wasn't. Not right now.

"I don't need you to figure anything out for me, Chaz. I knew this was a mistake from the start. I lost my focus and I—"

He moved so that they were now face-to-face instead of side by side. "Look me in the eye and tell me that you regret every moment we've spent together. Tell me that you weren't thinking about us having a future together just yesterday. Tell me, Riley."

She looked him in the eye—those warm brown eyes that always stared back at her with such caring and understanding. The words were in her mind but she couldn't say them. She couldn't bring herself to lie.

"I do not regret anything that we've done. We're adults and we decided to sleep together. I'm fine with that and I hope you are, too. But that's done now, Chaz. The affair is over and we can both get back to our respective lives."

He didn't look as if she'd slapped him this time, but he did stare at her in disbelief. She hoped he wouldn't continue to press this issue. She'd told him that she believed him—what else did he want? It didn't matter because Riley had nothing else to give.

"Yeah," he said finally. "We can get back to our respective lives."

"Great." That was a relief. She rubbed her hands down her skirt and moved to sit in her chair. "Good luck with your show this weekend and with the app. I really do wish you much success."

His lips were drawn in a tight line as he continued to stare at her. "Same to you, Riley. I wish you the best of whatever you're courageous enough to reach for."

He didn't wait for her response but left her office, closing the door quietly behind him.

Riley sat back in her chair and closed her eyes. If she kept them closed she wouldn't think about what she'd just done or how all those dreams she'd had this weekend had walked out the door. She wouldn't think about the man who'd just told her he was in love with her, or the fact that she was certain she'd fallen in love with him, too.

CHAPTER EIGHTEEN

TOBIAS SLAMMED THE phone down so hard it skipped over the base and he had to fiddle with the receiver to finally get it down correctly. When that was done, he slammed his palms on his desk and cursed fluently.

Chaz had walked into his uncle's office five minutes ago, catching the tail end of a one-sided conversation, but he could guess what it was about.

"That was the detective. We're pressing charges against Lenzo for stealing our product, which was the dress he made, and Ron's pressing charges against the receptionist at RGF who gave Lenzo the original design used for the dress. They'll both be charged with theft. From what the detective told me, she didn't waste any time confessing. Seems Lenzo was dating her specifically to get information. I could wring that idiot's neck right now!"

Chaz rubbed a finger over his chin. Once he'd recalled Lenzo's hostility on Friday and then again on Monday when Tobias fired him, Chaz figured the guy would have had to make only one phone call to get that story on the front page on Tuesday morning. When Chaz had left Riley's office on Tuesday, he'd gone straight to the police to share his suspicions and they'd immediately followed up.

"Exactly. But the pictures… Lenzo said he bought those from the reporter who was fired after Ron's tirade last week over an article the guy wrote."

The article about Walt's fiancée. Chaz cursed just like his uncle had.

"Can't trust anybody these days." Tobias sat back in his chair and scrubbed his hands over his face. "Well, we've got a big night tonight so we have to put this behind us."

"Got it." Chaz agreed that tonight was a big night. As far as putting all this behind them, that was easier said than done.

"Your launch went well last night. Heard you got a record number of downloads or something like that."

"Yeah, over forty-seven million in the first twelve hours." The number was still incredulous to him. "The quick influx of downloads caused a few glitches but we were able to work those out fairly quickly. So it looks like a success."

One Chaz hadn't been able to enjoy. Valeria had decided to post his interview, after all, highlighting the parts where he insisted ChatMe was not a dating service. That was where she'd added the rumors that the social media playboy had finally fallen in love with his family's number one enemy. Chaz had been tempted to call her and give her a piece of his mind. In the end, he'd refrained because what she'd published was true.

With that tidbit of knowledge, Chaz had left the office late last night and spent the rest of his launch day sitting in his apartment staring at the blinds he'd closed over all his windows because it reminded him of Riley.

"What do you plan on doing once this showing is over?"

Chaz shrugged. Working with his uncle had always been temporary, until the new men's brand was launched successfully; now he pondered what his next step would be. "Hadn't thought about it."

"You were always a piss-poor liar, son." Tobias chuckled and crossed his leg to rest an ankle on the opposite knee.

"Really. I haven't thought about when I'll head back to Miami." Or *if* he would return to the life he'd had before coming to New York. For a minute, Chaz had thought there might be a reason for him to permanently relocate here.

He could easily work remotely from Manhattan or open another office in the city. One that could be used specifically as the ChatMe headquarters. But that plan had stalled in the water on Tuesday morning.

"And why is that? Because you got cozy with Riley Gold?"

The glare he sent his uncle must have expressed everything Chaz was feeling about him mentioning her name.

"Whoa there, don't get defensive. I'm not calling her a thief anymore. You got to the bottom of all that foolishness. Which is why I'm gonna shoot straight with you right now." Tobias smoothed down his tie.

"You've been walking around here with a long face all week. Last time I saw you looking like that was when that little boy you liked having over the house moved away."

"His name was Caleb and we were twelve when his family moved back to India." He'd been the closest thing Chaz ever had to a sibling or a family member his age.

"Right. Well, anyway, that's how you've been looking. Like you've lost your best friend."

Tobias had no idea how true those words were. Chaz had told Riley things he'd never shared with anyone. She knew him better than even his uncle did. She knew the real Chaz. And had walked away from him.

"I should get over to the venue," Chaz said and started to stand.

"I'm not finished. Sit down."

Chaz reluctantly did what he was told.

"You went and fell in love with a woman who you know you shouldn't have." Tobias held up a hand when Chaz was about to speak. "And she shouldn't have fallen for you, either. Both of you knew better. You knew about the bad blood between me and Ron and, in turn, our families. But you went and did it, anyway. There's only one explanation for that."

Chaz leaned forward and frowned. "An explanation for falling in love?"

"No. An explanation for why, despite the odds and family members you knew would be against you, that you and Riley still found your way to each other. It's called fate."

"Come on, Unc. Don't start with that nonsense."

"Call it what you want, but if there's one thing I know it's love."

Chaz laughed. He couldn't help it. "You? The man's whose been married eight times wants me to believe he knows about love."

"I do. That's precisely why I've been married eight times. You see people out here running around believing that you only get one chance. You fall in love and if for whatever reason you don't stay there, you don't get to try again. But you do."

"And that's your motto. Keep trying again and again until you get it right?"

Tobias shook his head. "You get it right for the time it lasts. That's all you can be worried about.

Tomorrow is not promised, so take what you can get now. My father used to tell me and your mother that. Why do you think she ran off and married your father when she was only eighteen instead of going to college? She was taking my father's advice and now I'm giving that advice to you."

"What are you saying?" Tobias had mentioned his mother and Chaz knew he was referring to Riley when he talked about love. The only two women to ever occupy space in his heart were being tossed in his face right now and Chaz didn't know how much longer he'd be able to remain civil.

"If you love that woman, fight for her. Go through whatever hoops she wants you to, dance to her beat, stand up to her father and those Gold boys, but whatever you do don't give up. The reason I keep getting more shots at love is simple, Chaz—I'm smart enough to remain open and available for it to find me. Now, if you're smart like I believe you are, you'll accept that love has found you and you'll do whatever it takes to hold on to it."

Tobias's words played over and over in Chaz's mind throughout the night and the celebration for their show and into the weekend when celebrations continued, but Chaz's heart still ached.

Tiny flakes of white confetti rained down over the crowd as ten models wearing the first wedding gowns in the Golden Bride Collection traipsed the runway for a second time to a standing ovation. Following right behind them and walking like super-models themselves were the three women designers and Riley.

They'd grabbed her backstage and insisted she come out with them to celebrate what her vision had created. The designers wore all-white ensembles while Riley had selected a wine-colored pant-suit and gold pumps for this evening's show. Her smile was genuine, spreading across her face until her cheeks hurt and her heart thumped wildly as her mind screamed, *You did it!*

Lifting an arm to wave at everyone in the audience, Riley and the designers took a bow before turning and walking back. Her father and RJ were up next. Both dressed in dark suits and walking as if they, too, owned the runway, the Gold men gave the crowd their handsome smiles and appreciative waves.

But the moment Riley stepped down into the backstage area she was pulled into a tight embrace.

"I am so damn proud of you, Riley! So very proud!"

Riley pulled back and kissed her mother's cheek. "Thank you, Mom. Thank you so much!"

The Gold women hugged once more and then Marva eased her daughter away from the cheers, high fives and other celebratory reactions going on backstage. They stopped in front of one of the model tables all the way toward the back door and Marva took both her daughter's hands, bringing them up to kiss.

Her mother was a beautiful woman with a glowing tawny-brown complexion and thick silver-streaked hair that fell to her shoulders in big, heavy curls. Marva wore a cream-and-gold organza gown from the RGold couture collection.

She smiled brightly at her daughter. "I knew you would find your space and shine as brightly as the star you were meant to be." Marva's eyes glistened with unshed tears.

"Thank you, Mom, for always believing in me. I couldn't have done any of this without knowing that you were in my corner."

Marva shook her head. "Yes, you could have. You were meant to do this. Your father may be the designer in this family and RJ the face that can sell anything we produce, but you, Riley, are the brains behind this company. Your analytical mind is what brought this entire collection to fruition. You saw the need, carved out a unique niche for our brand and soared with it. You, my baby, have done well."

For the first time in days Riley felt full. Warmth spread from her chest to her cheeks and she squeezed her mother's hands to hold on to all the emotion brewing inside. This was the moment she'd been waiting for—the validation she hadn't realized she'd fought so hard to receive. While it wasn't her father or even RJ for that matter, this was so much better. For some reason it meant more to have her mother—the woman who had always been Riley's role model—say she'd done well.

"You know what would make this moment better, my darling?"

Oh no, Marva had slipped in a "my darling." The nicknames her parents used for her had at one point seemed endearing. Now, as she knocked on the door of turning thirty, she'd learned those endearments usually came with pieces of parental advice she either didn't want to accept or just didn't want to hear. Tonight, Riley feared both were about to come.

"What's that? All the champagne we're going to drink at the after-party?"

As much as Marva loved good champagne, Riley knew that wasn't what her mother was referring to.

"If you could celebrate two major accomplishments in your life at the same time."

When Riley would have turned away, her mother held on to her hands. "Oh no, that's enough running away, don't you think?"

"I'm not running away. That's not what I do, remember?" Riley had stood taller, squaring her shoulders as she stared back at her mother. The actions had come instinctively.

Marva could only shake her head. "My brave, cautious little girl. You've always fought for every inch, haven't you?"

Riley resisted the urge to shrug but said, "I had to."

Her mother pursed her lips and gave Riley a knowing nod. "That was your father's fault for making you feel like you had to be even better than the boys. And my fault for not cutting Ron off earlier with that foolish behavior."

"It's nobody's fault," Riley said. Her father's apology had come on Tuesday evening, after her mother had apparently spent the better part of that morning yelling at him for the way he'd yelled at Riley. In addition to being fashion royalty, her parents were pretty good at yelling and then making up later.

"Nonsense. If we hadn't let you believe that all you needed to be happy in life was to succeed in your career you wouldn't be in the predicament you're in now."

Riley attempted another smile. "I'm not in a predicament, Mom. I'm actually in the most wonderful moment of my life. We should get out front—I'm sure the reporters are swarming."

That last remark completely gave away Riley's fake bravado and she saw the moment her mother basked in the small triumph. Riley could do nothing but sigh.

"It's okay to love him." Marva's voice was softer now, but Riley could still hear her over all the celebrating going on around them. "You don't have to feel like you're going against some ridiculous family honor."

"I should have known better."

"Nonsense. You should have done exactly what you did, reached for the love you deserve. If you love him, Riley, and he loves and respects you, that's all that matters. None of this—not the accolades at work, my or your father's validation or any amount of money—is ever going to be worth it if you don't have someone you love to share it with."

"Not every woman needs a man, Mom. We're so beyond that in this century."

"You need love. I don't care what anybody says, you will always need love. Whether it's from a man, woman or alien, you need to feel like you're loved and respected for something other than the job you do. You need to feel that you, just being you, is enough to be celebrated."

Riley had only felt that way once, or rather each time she was with Chaz. He never looked at her as Riley Gold, daughter of Ron Gold and his uncle's archenemy. He'd told her from the start of their affair that they were not the feud.

"I pushed him away." The admission that had burned in her throat for the past few days came in a soft whisper and Riley looked away, blinking furiously to keep tears from falling.

Marva released her hands, touching a finger to her daughter's chin and turning her head so that she could look into Riley's face. "Go back and get him."

It was a simple statement…one that echoed in

Riley's mind like her mother had shouted it through a bullhorn. But that was impossible, at least right now. Her father and brothers were headed their way and the celebration in the old historic building they'd rented in NoHo for the show was about to be jumping with the Gold after-party.

An hour later, loud music combined with three glasses of champagne had given Riley another headache that she wished would go away. The party was in full swing and she'd managed to find a quiet corner to hide for a few moments.

She'd already spoken to fashion editors, posed for pictures with some of tonight's models and nibbled on whatever hors d'oeuvres her mother had whizzed by and popped into her mouth.

"Be gracious. Keep smiling. Sell the product." Ron had kissed her on the forehead in between giving his instructions. "And remember that I love you, my daughter. No matter how foolish I can be it's just because I love you."

Riley recalled the moment her father had found her after his walk on the runway and it made her smile. Her father was always going to have her heart.

With that thought Riley reached for another glass of champagne from the tray held by a server. She took a small sip and was grateful for having something to hold in her hands, which hadn't stopped shaking all night. Her mother's words played on loop in her mind. Those and the words Chaz had said to her that day he'd left her standing in her office.

Lights continued to shift with the beat of the music and the hundreds of guests they'd invited to the show danced and ate and drank their way into Fashion Week bliss while Riley stood by watching. That was when she saw him.

He walked through the door across the room wearing a dark-colored suit and button-front shirt open at the neck. One of his hands was in the front pocket of his pants as he stood there looking around the room, and Riley immediately pushed away from the wall where she'd been leaning.

Her heart beat to the rhythm of the fast-paced music and her fingers gripped the stem of her glass. He was here. Chaz had come to the RGF after-party when he hadn't received an invitation.

She could leave now. Her clever little hiding place was adjacent to the exit door. All she had to do was take a few steps, push the bar on that door and she'd be free. But she didn't do that, because freedom wasn't waiting on the other side of that exit door; it was just more time in the shelter she'd created for herself after believing she wasn't worthy of love.

Riley took a step forward. She inhaled deeply and let the breath out slowly, reminding herself that she could do this. She'd proved herself to her family and the fashion world tonight, surely she could walk across this room and talk to one man. She took another step and a server almost bumped into her. Riley set her glass on the tray this new server carried and continued her trek across the room.

Chaz had walked down the few stairs from the entry and was now moving in the opposite direction. He seemed to be looking around the room, searching for someone. Riley's heart beat faster and she picked up her pace, pushing past the people cluttering the floor until she saw Chaz walk into the lounge. She excused herself and hurried toward that space, fearful that Chaz would find another exit and leave.

She bumped into a photographer seconds before stepping into the lounge area and he held on to her waist to keep her from falling.

"I'm sorry," Riley said, her hands going to the guy's shoulders.

"No problem," the guy told her and turned them around so that she was now standing in the lounge area and he was headed to the dance floor.

Riley was just about to resume her search for Chaz when she felt him right behind her. It was that heat that only they shared that warned of his proximity. The smoldering hunger that always started in the pit of her stomach before spreading throughout her body.

"Hi, Riley."

His voice draped over her like a warm blanket and Riley turned slowly.

"Hi, Chaz."

"Can we talk?"

"Definitely." And because neither of them moved for the seconds after that brief exchange, Riley grabbed Chaz's hand and pulled him through the lounge area and out into the front foyer.

There was significantly less noise and fewer people here.

"I was wrong," Riley said the moment they stopped walking.

She released Chaz's hand and looked at his surprised expression.

"I knew you wouldn't steal from me and I should have spoken up. I should have been adamant about that and about who you are. But I was afraid. I thought it was happening all over again. The betrayal and the scandal—I felt like it was all coming back and I didn't know how to handle that."

"I would never betray you, Riley. And despite how much it seems like I love the spotlight or being the subject of reports on my love life, that's not who I am, either."

She knew that. Riley was certain she knew exactly who Chaz was.

"I saw your uncle's press conference about the arrests. I'm sorry this had to happen." Tobias King had stated unequivocally that he did not condone any type of treachery or games being played with his business or RGF's. That was not the method of competition he wanted. Riley believed him, too.

"I talked to your brother."

Riley blinked in confusion. "What? Who? When?"

"RJ. He showed up at my apartment the night after the press conference. He's the one who gave me the invitation to your show."

She didn't know what to say. How had RJ known she would want to see Chaz tonight?

It didn't matter. Riley took a step closer to Chaz.

"I love you," she said, feeling waves of relief course through her body at the admission. "I should have admitted it the day you were in my office telling me that you would take care of the scandal. I should have trusted myself and my feelings, but I couldn't. I didn't know how. I should have—"

Riley's words were cut short as Chaz cupped her cheeks and leaned closer. "You should kiss me, Riley."

He paused after saying the words as if waiting for her to decide. There were people in the foyer with them—not a lot but some. They could be photographers or reporters or models, or anybody else who would love to continue spreading the rumor that Riley Gold was having an affair with Chaz Warren regardless of their family feud.

For the first time Riley didn't give a damn. People could say and print whatever they wanted. She was going to reach for what she wanted and to hell with anyone who didn't approve.

"Yeah, I should kiss you," she whispered and leaned closer to touch her lips to his.

* * * * *

COMING SOON!

We really hope you enjoyed reading this book. If you're looking for more romance, be sure to head to the shops when new books are available on

Thursday 23rd January

To see which titles are coming soon, please visit **millsandboon.co.uk/nextmonth**

LET'S TALK

Romance

For exclusive extracts, competitions
and special offers, find us online:

MILLS & BOON

MODERN

Power and Passion

Prepare to be swept off your feet by sophisticated, sexy and seductive heroes, in some of the world's most glamourous and romantic locations, where power and passion collide.